A VALENTINE TREAT FOR YOU!

Leisure Books is pleased to present this collection of Valentine stories by three of today's bestselling contemporary romance writers!

PARRIS AFTON BONDS
"Written in the Stars"

When her nightlife turned into a nightmare, Sarah almost gave up hope of finding a man. But when she took up tennis, her lonely single life was soon spiced up by a game of mixed doubles she'd never forget.

RITA CLAY ESTRADA
"The Magic Time Machine"

Theresa had always dreamed of traveling back in time to see what life would have been like with an old boyfriend. But it wasn't until she visited J.D.'s nightclub and took an imaginary leap to the past that she turned all her fantasies into passionate reality.

LYNDA TRENT
"Branson's Daughter"

Desperate to escape a no-win situation, Hannah moved away from her hometown right after her high school graduation. But fifteen years later, she returned to bury her past—and to build a future with the boy she had always loved.

Parris Afton Bonds

Rita Clay Estrada

Lynda Trent

Valentine Sampler

LEISURE BOOKS   **NEW YORK CITY**

A LEISURE BOOK®

January 1993

Published by

Dorchester Publishing Co., Inc.
276 Fifth Avenue
New York, NY 10001

Printed in the United States of America.

WRITTEN IN THE STARS
Parris Afton Bonds

For Dale Brannaka,
who is starlight and sun warmth.

Chapter One

February 14—Valentine's Day, and I am alone. I am waiting, Soul Mate. Where are you?

With a sigh, Sarah put down her pen and dog-eared journal. When two years ago she was made junior partner at her law firm for $80,000 a year, she had begun to feel an inner panic.

Ever since she decided to become an attorney, she had worried that she might not get the raises and promotions for which she had worked so hard. Now, she was worried that she would. That she would be locked in to that professional ladder climbing. A ladder that never ran out of rungs.

She had started recording in a journal as a daily exercise to monitor her feelings. To give her a clue as to what it was she was searching for. She picked up the red leather-bound journal again and flipped back through the pages. Different colored inks and drab gray pencil lead caught her eye.

So, too, did the varied styles of her penmanship. Here, an entry was neat and precise. A couple of pages earlier, an entry was scrawled. Here, large and determined. There, small, tight, and fearful.

One page sported a muddy brown smear. She glanced at the date and remembered that was the period when she had gone on a chocolate binge— right after she had learned that her old boyfriend, Craig, had married.

"There's more to life, Sarah, than how much money you make or how much corporate prestige you have," he had told her that last day they were together. She had been dedicated and proud of all she had achieved, and his words had stung.

Looking back, she wondered why he had not seen that she had been a reflection of him, that he, too, had been more interested in a partnership than a relationship. Apparently, he had changed no more than she. The last she had heard, he had made senior partner in a big-eight accounting firm—and had divorced six months later.

She was glad now that she had not given into Craig when he had first asked her to marry him. Something, she didn't know what, had seemed to be missing in their relationship.

Something was missing now, all right. She didn't have a life.

She turned several more pages in her journal. Some of them had blurred script in spots, the result of unchecked tears. This one, for example.

An earlier entry:

January 28—Turned thirty-four today. Still no real food in the refrigerator. There must be . . . a splotch here . . . to life. I want . . . another splotch . . . to discover the self I denied for the fast career track.

Some of the entries had been too painful to reveal at that particular moment. They had been metaphors like this one:

January 4—The townhouse walls are bare. The frames of Craig's paintings have left their yellowed silhouettes. Perhaps I'll find the right paintings to liven up my walls.

She never did find the "perfect" paintings she had imagined would replace the ones Craig had taken with him. Never enough time to browse through the art stores.

For the last eight years her life had been typified by returning home at eleven o'clock at night after a day of a breakfast of champions—a jolt of java—power lunching, leaving work at six-thirty to have drinks with one client, followed by dinner with another, then going home, exhausted, with briefs to be reviewed before the next day's 9 A.M. conferences, when the whole merciless treadmill would begin again.

Well, work would no longer be her *raîson d'etre.*

She glanced at the clock. Almost seven. She really didn't want to do this—play tennis with that man from church. What was his name? She must be consciously blocking it out. She flipped forward to yesterday's entry.

February 13—Joe Smith, the man I met in the church bookstore, called. Wanted to know if I would like to play tennis tomorrow night after work. I should never have given him my phone number. But we got into discussing metaphysics, then mind control, then using it on commonplace things like tennis. I made it clear to him this wasn't a date. I hope I made it clear. Just fun, just taking time to smell the roses. I can't remember what the man looks like. Homely, I think. Oh, God, I wish I hadn't agreed to this.

Maybe not homely, she thought when she opened her front door to greet him. But plain. Definitely plain. A round face. Short, only a little taller than she. And balding.

What else could you expect when you reached the mid-forties? Your age definitely showed. And life's disappointments. The forties were mid-life crisis time. Except she was reaching her crisis time far too early. It showed in her hollowed eyes and taut, feelingless smile. She was burned out. That was all.

She smiled brightly. "I hope the courts are dry." So much rain had fallen in the last week that she almost had had to wade through water to reach her townhouse door.

"We can always go for coffee and just talk," he suggested.

That smacked too much of dating. She didn't want to lead him on. He didn't interest her in that way. "The apartment courts should be dry."

For a while she and Joe just batted the ball back and forth, then they played a game. She was glad he had suggested tennis. You didn't have to worry about making small talk. Until you changed sides.

"Good serving." Couldn't she think of anything clever to say?

"So why won't you date?" Joe asked.

She wiped the perspiration from her temple. "Too busy. Besides, I'm not interested in settling down." Not unless there really was such a thing as a soul mate. Someone who complemented her in every way. She had always thought herself practical and prosaic, but lately her daydreams were those of a far-fetched romantic.

His brows lifted. They, like his hair, were blond. She had never gone for blond men. "At thirty-four, you're not ready?"

"We have nothing in common, age to begin with. You're forty-three, aren't you?"

He grinned. "I didn't ask you for a date. Remember, this is just a friendly tennis game."

Relief flowed through her. "Yeah, just friends."

"Your serve."

She took the two balls he proffered on his racket and watched him walk to the far court. Great legs. Great buns.

*   *   *

"I'm telling you, Marge, I don't want to do this."

Her paralegal at Bernstein, Raftiff, & Richmond turned her BMW's steering wheel into the parking lot of Rumors. "Nonsense, if you are going to experience life, this is the place to start."

"At a place like this, I feel like a used car in a repo auction."

Marge flicked her an assessing glance. The paralegal's reassuring smile was a little weak. "Next time, Sarah, why don't you try wearing something that isn't so—uh—businesslike. I mean those power suits of yours are fine for intimidating the opposition in a courtroom but defense is not what you want here. Attraction is the name of the game."

Why had she agreed to this? If she didn't like these singles clubs, then the kind of man she was interested in wouldn't either.

Give it a chance, Sarah. Maybe some beleaguered male got roped into coming here, also.

Still, it was so humiliating. To her, at least. So why was she doing this?

Because I am lonely. Lonely way deep inside. And no amount of socializing seems to cure this ache.

"You need to do more fun things," Marge continued as she pulled the car up next to a pickup, one of many scattered throughout the parking lot. The battered truck told Sarah that Rumors' customers belonged mostly to the younger, country-western crowd. "And fun things don't include business lunches and dinners. You need to feel like a woman again. Craig wasn't the only man in the cosmos who can do that for you, you know."

"I know you're right, Marge. Lately the conviction that there must be something more to life has been overwhelming."

"When your lifestyle is as dry as a raisin, then it's party time."

With a sigh, Sarah slipped her alligator purse strap over her shoulder and followed Marge across the parking lot. Inside the remodeled hacienda-style building, the lights were dim and the music blaring.

A dozen or more men's heads swiveled at the latest arrivals on the scene, then turned back to watch the gyrating couples on the strobe-lit dance floor. The thud-thud-thud of a base guitar echoed her heart. The indifference of the men reiterated the indifference she felt about her life in general. That was one of the reasons she had started going back to church, to seek the answer to the plaguing question of what life was all about.

She slid onto a tall stool, one of three at a small, round table and peered through the acrid cigarette smoke. "Remember, you said only one hour."

Marge was already smiling at a man with a gray mustache and beard, who was returning the smile. Freckled, with red-orange short curly hair and blue eyes, Marge caught one's eye. She had

Parris Afton Bonds

been single for five years and knew the game—
whatever that was between male and female.
Sarah grimaced. Obviously, she hadn't figured
out the rules or the game yet.

Disgusted with herself, she took a hasty swallow
of her margarita and choked on a glob of salt. She
coughed so hard that she lost her balance and
would have toppled backwards had not a passing
body served as a bulwark. The body, a man's, stag-
gered. Blindly, she grasped at anything to break
her fall. The man's tie served her purpose. Her
frantic grip jerked him around and hauled him
against the table.

"Oh, God!" she wheezed. "I'm sorry." Her eyes
smarted with tears.

"Woman, you're dangerous."

Other people were staring. She wanted to slink
under the table, but his body was in her way. She
glanced down and saw that the portion of his tie
below her fist was draped in her margarita glass.
"Oh, I'm so sorry."

He removed his soggy tie from her grasp. "It's
all right—if I can just get out of here."

She was mortified. "No, no, you don't have to
do that. I was leaving."

Marge stared at her with astonishment. "We
just got here. And we came in my car."

"Oh, yeah," she mumbled.

The smile on his face eased her embarrassment.
"Come on, we both need to get out of here."

He definitely wasn't her type. Too good-looking.

14

Too smooth. "I don't think so."

"I thought coffee stains might also look good on my tie. Want a cup?"

She had to give him credit. He was determined—and clever. "I don't think so."

"Go on." Marge laughed and nudged her shoulder. "You're safe with him. I can tell a gentleman when I see one."

Bemused, Sarah stared back at the attractive face. With chestnut hair silvered at his temples, he appeared somewhere in his forties. Brown eyes smiled back at her. "Well?"

Nothing. No chemistry. She shook her head. "No, I don't think so," she repeated for the third time. "I'm busy right now." Why did she feel she had to offer an explanation?

His smile was non-threatening. "Good. Tomorrow is not right now. May I call you then?"

"Her number is 555-5622."

She shot Marge a blistering look.

His eyes flicked from Marge back to her, his gaze questioning.

"Her name is Sarah," Marge put in again. "Sarah Logan."

His smile deepened, forming dimples. He really was handsome with strong features. "Well, Sarah Logan? I am Dwayne Fields. May I call you?"

She had to smile back. "All right." After all, she didn't have to accept a date. Talk, that was all she had to do, she told herself, as she watched him walk away.

What do you talk about? she asked herself the next day as she kicked off her heels and with a sigh settled into her wicker rocker. All she knew was business talk. Besides, the man didn't do anything for her. Didn't make her tingle the way a soul mate should.

A wine cooler. That was what she wanted. But she was too tired to get up and go to the refrigerator. Work had been a hellhole that day, with a case she had pleaded being lost as well as a ruling overturned. The dismal, rainy afternoon had not helped her mood.

The ringing phone made her start. It might be her mother, who would talk forty-five minutes about how important a career was for a woman and that a woman never knew when the man in her life might abandon her. At least, that was the general tone of her mother's conversations. Her mother had never trusted men, not since her own husband had run off with another woman when Sarah had been three years old.

The phone rang twice more before she found the energy to answer it. "Sarah? This is Dwayne. Dwayne Fields. From Rumors."

"Yes, I remember."

"How are you doing?"

"I'm fine. How is your tie?"

He laughed. "It will recover. I won't."

"Oh?" *Come on, Sarah, you can do better than that. You've pled cases before the toughest judge in town. This can't be any worse.*

16

"All I've been able to think about the last twenty-four hours is a brunette with the loveliest green eyes and soft, warm smile."

"Oh."

"Sarah, telephone chitchat doesn't come easily for me. Would you meet me for coffee somewhere tomorrow night? You don't work on Friday nights, too, do you?"

"No, not usually." Should she accept? Marge said she spent too much time by herself.

Twenty-four hours later, she was driving her Mercedes into The River View Cafe's parking lot. Being successful meant keeping up an image that included one's mode of transportation. She was beginning to dislike her image.

Her stomach felt nervous. She took a deep breath, got out of her car, and walked toward the neon-lit entrance, at the same time straightening her jacket lapel. She had chosen the black silk trouser suit because it was casual yet trendy. Black communicated more than power and sophistication. It breathed mystery.

Dwayne was inside. He looked taller than she remembered and even more handsome in a white V-neck sweater and gray slacks. "Good evening." Her voice was firm and crisp and as impersonal as that of a district attorney.

"Hi." His gaze was admiring. "Take your coffee straight or with a splash of cream?"

She managed a smile. "I take my cream with a splash of coffee and too much sugar."

A teenaged waitress seated them in a booth with a view of the rain-dappled bayou. A family of five were seated nearby. The booths on either side of her and Dwayne were empty. Everything and everyone seemed so normal. Yet here she was with a stranger, a man who was interested in knowing more about her. The prospect was unnerving.

"You ever been married?" he asked.

She swallowed a sip of her coffee. It was tepid. "Never. And you?"

"I was married for fifteen years."

"That's a long time."

"You bet." His smile was engaging. "Especially when you're miserable. My ex was a real bitch."

She flinched. She could never accept that the failure of a relationship was solely the fault of one partner. She had failed Craig as much as he had her. They had both opted for perk-filled powerful positions at the expense of a relationship that had become hollow. No, had always been hollow but had offered security. Fortunately, he had had what she hadn't: the courage to end the farce.

Dwayne turned a determined gaze on her. "Surely, there's been a special man in your life?"

"Not for the last two years."

"Oh, then, you're just getting back in the market."

"Market?

"You know. The dating scene."

Of course. Her finger traced the rim of her cup. His nails, she noticed, were manicured. She thought of Joe Smith, with his square hands, callused by his hobby, carpentry. "Let's just say that I am finally coming to realize that devotion to myself is more important than devotion to my company. I'm taking more time for my personal life."

"I can see you're a bright woman. What do you do for a living?"

She glanced up at him to see if his words were sincere. His expression was open enough. "Practice law."

Nothing, no expression of interest in her profession from his side.

Maybe attorneys made him nervous. "What do you do?"

He brightened. "Bullshit."

"What?"

"I write copy for Whittier Advertising."

"I take it you don't enjoy your job?"

"The people can be real bores. Advertising is mostly female-oriented. Some of the women I deal with are on real power trips. They think their business cards and job titles give them control over men."

The evening suddenly stretched interminably. Her coffee tasted acrid. Her spirits were like a popped balloon. She didn't know how she managed to keep up her end of the conversation for the next thirty minutes, but good-bye came easier.

19

*   *   *

February 21—Had first real date tonight in two years. He seemed to have so much going for him. And yet . . . What's wrong with me? Will I never find someone I can relate to?

Chapter Two

Sarah swung to the left and hit a smashing back-hand. She sent the ball hurtling cross court in a shot that Joe Smith wouldn't be able to return in a million years. A yell of triumph burst from her. Amazement at her own skill anchored her to the court's far left corner.

Then, incredibly, Joe lunged in what could only have been a Superman feat and popped the ball back into her court. The drop shot did just that—dropped just over the net, while she stood with her mouth open.

"Get your butt in gear, Logan!" Joe called, his eyes bright with laughter.

She had to grin back. "That was a cheap shot. Anyone can take the easy way out. It's keeping the ball in play that takes real skill."

He trotted up to the net. "Play. That's your whole problem."

"What?"

"You don't play enough."

She walked toward him, the net between them. Perspiration ran down her rib cage. Her breathing came hard. "What do you call this?"

"Well, *you* call it competition."

"What do *you* call it?"

"When *you* call it playing, then I'll be satisfied."

Sarah stared back at him in confusion. She made an exaggerated gesture of wiping her sweating palm on her warm-up suit. "Why should you care if I call it playing?"

He tossed her a ball, damp from a rain puddle on the court. "Because, as your friend, I don't think you take out enough time to enjoy yourself."

"What do you suggest?"

"A good romp."

She was waiting for him to add "with me."

He didn't.

Why did she feel she was holding out on him by not telling him she had had a date? After all, she and Joe were merely friends. Her eyes narrowed. "Just what does that mean—romp?"

He shrugged and started walking back toward the receiving line. "Whatever the dictionary says," he threw over his shoulder.

When she got back to her apartment, she looked up the word. "High-spirited and boisterous play;

an episode of lovemaking."

She lay alone in her king-sized bed that night—once hers and Craig's—and gave consideration to Joe's suggestion. Maybe Joe had a point.

She thought about Chad Reese at work. The company's CPA seemed serious but occasionally told a joke, assuring her of a sense of humor. Though not as handsome as Dwayne, he did have a certain something that had attracted her. With her workload, she hadn't given him much thought. Now her memory turned on her mind's projector.

His curly brown hair was grizzled with gray, and the glasses he wore imparted dignity, while setting off gorgeous brown eyes. He had a way of peering up from those glasses that could make a woman look twice.

He had flirted mildly right after she had begun working at Bernstein et al, but she had had no interest in dating then. She had been wholly committed to her work.

That following Monday she was in the company dining room when Chad Reese stopped by her table. The pin-stripe three-piece business suit made him look even more appealing.

He told her about his latest fiasco with his eighteen-year-old daughter, who lived with him. "We were both trying to get ready for dates at the same time and arguing over who got to use the hair dryer."

"I know what you mean. For a while, I lived with

my mother—the first two years I was in college. We were forever getting our clothing mixed up. It's tough when at the last moment you have to go looking for a blouse you were planning on wearing for a date."

"Then you do date?"

"I really haven't been dating that much."

"You're no longer involved with the man you were seeing . . . Craig somebody?"

So he knew about Craig. His interest pleased her. "Not for two years now." Those first weeks after she and Craig had parted, she had been barely able to get through each day. By bedtime, she counted it as another day she had survived. "It's taken me all this time to make up my mind if I really wanted to date again."

"The more you get out, the quicker you will heal. Relationships do that for you. Especially long-term ones, or so the therapists say."

Here was a man who seemed well adjusted, positive, stable. "I don't think I know how to handle a long-term relationship," she admitted.

He winked. "Sure you do. Just give it time. I don't want to scare you off, so how about a short-term movie Friday night?"

She laughed. "That sounds safe enough."

"After I check the entertainment section tonight, I'll call you about the movie."

He called her promptly at eight that night, and they discussed taxes, weather, in-laws, school systems, and his therapist. "He says to be sure to see the movie, *Black Depths*. It will give me real insights into my psyche."

March 2—Date with Chad Reese. He brought me a dazzling single rose. Said it was for a short-stemmed beauty. That should have been all he said. But when I pricked my finger on one of the rose's thorns, he commented that it was supposedly a sign that my subconscious was seeking pain. That I wanted to be hurt.

What a red flag!

We went to a Chevy Chase flick and dinner afterward at a small, suburban seafood restaurant. When he brought me home, I let him kiss me. Mistake. Nothing. No passion, no feeling at all. What is wrong with me? Somewhere along the map of my life, I have lost the passion for living. Or did I ever really possess it?

Sarah whacked at the tennis ball, putting it into play. "I took your advice."

Joe batted the ball back to her at 120 mph. "What was that?"

She returned the torpedo. "I took out time to enjoy myself. I went to the movies. I had a date."

With another effortless swing, he put the ball back in her court. "So, how did the movie go?"

Her arm vibrated. Did her racket still have strings? "The movie went fine." The warm-up was working the kinks out of her body. She really looked forward to Wednesdays and the exercise.

He whammed the ball back to her forehand. "And the date?"

She took her frustration out in a solid whack at the ball. "The date was definitely not a romp."

"Why not?" he called back.

She dashed to the net to field a short return. "I couldn't relate to him. We talked mostly about his therapy. Like his shock treatment last year, among other things. For depression."

"Definitely not a good indication for someone you want to have a romp with. You'll know if it's right. It'll be wall-socket sex."

She had to grin at that. "So, now what?" She batted a net ball. "Find someone I can discuss more substantial subjects with? Like world religions or something?"

He trotted up to the other side of the net and pounced on her attempt at a passing shot. "Do you know how you feel about religion?"

She stopped, and his ball went by her. "Well, no. That's a good question, Joe. I don't know what I feel anymore about anything. What do you feel? About religion? About God?"

His high forehead furrowed. His large fingers toyed thoughtfully with his racket strings. "I didn't know how I felt about anything either, until I lost three years of my life."

Was he putting her on? "What are you talking about, Joe?"

His blue eyes, deep and clear as the Caribbean, fastened on her. "I was a professor at the University of Lebanon nine years ago, when I was taken as a political hostage. For three years I never saw sunlight or starlight or moonlight."

At that instant she felt the wonderful warmth of the sun, even though it was the last rays before sundown. She missed the sunlight by working inside a cold office building from sunup until sundown.

She had known that he taught at the local college, but his lack of drive had puzzled her. With his energy and intelligence, she would have expected him to be further up the ladder of achievement. "So that's why your freedom is so important to you?"

"Yes. I'll never understand why it happened, being taken hostage, but at this point in my life I can honestly say I am glad it did. I learned things I never would have otherwise. I realize now that I had taken my life for granted. Now every moment is exciting."

That was what had been missing in her life—excitement! "What else did you learn?"

"I learned that I had also taken my wife and three children for granted."

Her mouth nearly dropped open with astonishment. "You are married?"

"I was. When I was finally released, I found that I had changed drastically. So had my wife. We had nothing left in common except our love for our children. We divorced."

"I'm sorry. I think a failed marriage must hurt

even more than the death of a spouse." Maybe that's why she had never married. Maybe because of her drive, her intense need to succeed, she was afraid of failing.

"There are no failures. Only beginnings and endings, Sarah."

She sighed. "I used to think I had all the answers. Now I know I don't know anything."

He smiled. "For every question, there is an answer. Einstein or somebody said that. We just have to keep looking."

"So I just keep looking for Mr. Wonderful?"

"Mr. Right. I doubt he'll be wonderful all the time. Sure, keep looking."

March 15—I've accepted a date with Lance Wilson. Met him at a Friends of Friends Party. He was always cracking a joke. At least he'll keep the conversation going.

"I have a date next Friday night." Sarah buttoned her white shorts and headed for the living room.

Joe glanced up from one of the paperbacks he had selected from her bookcase, a book on embracing the inner self. "Is this Mr. Right?"

"I don't know." She sat down on the couch and tugged on one white sock. She had been late getting away from the office for her standing Wednesday tennis game. "I met him at one of those Friends of Friends parties. He's a pilot for a major airline. And he's younger than I am."

Joe wedged the paperback back into its space between *A Crack in the Cosmic Egg* and *The Tao of Physics*. It was obvious to Joe that Sarah loved to read. "Is that a problem for you? The age gap?"

Her brow wrinkled. "I'm not sure. The women's movement says no, but I wonder whether we'll be on the same wave length."

He chuckled. "Where is he taking you?"

She laced up her tennis shoe. "To the Pepper Mill. I've never been there."

"You'll like it. It's an old abandoned mill converted to an Italian restaurant." He selected another book and flipped through it. "What attracted you to him?"

She began tying her other shoe. "You know, I never considered that. Maybe his jokes."

From between those golden stubby eyelashes, Joe's blue eyes studied her thoughtfully. "A lot of men tell jokes, Sarah. This man must have something else that connects with you."

"No." His pensive gaze caused her to stop and think. She propped her arm on her bare knee and rested her chin in her palm. "Not really. I mean it's not like we share any common interests. Not anything I've discovered yet, anyway."

Joe held up the book, cover outward. *The Eternal Now.* "Good book. The author surprised me. Made me really stretch my thinking."

She headed for her bedroom mirror. "I haven't had a chance to read it yet." She grasped her riotous curls and tucked them into a clasp atop her head. "Between church and tennis and dating, I've been too busy."

"Getting a personal life, are you?" he called from the living room.

With surprise, she stared back at her reflection. "Why, yes, I guess I am."

March 16—Lance Wilson was full of jokes, short on substance. And definitely not interested in serious matters. He didn't even bother to walk me to the door. I have the distinct impression that he asked me out because he thought I was one of those older females desperate for a male. I give up. Soul mates don't exist, except in a romantic's foolish fantasy. And I'm too old for foolish fantasy.

"I don't know, Marge. I think there is definitely something wrong with my libido."

"Why, because you didn't feel like going to bed with that guy you met at one of those Friends of Friends parties? You're not going to click with every man, Sarah."

She swallowed a sip of her wine cooler, straight out of the bottle. "I haven't connected with any of them," she said, realizing she had used one of Joe's verbs. "Connect." She rolled the word around in her mind. The verb said a lot when applied to relations.

"Did you—with Craig—connect, I mean?"

She closed her eyes and tried to visualize

scenes of intimacy from the three years they had spent together. But mostly scenes of silence, of noncommunication flickered behind her lids. Those nights spent lying side by side with Craig, unspoken thoughts a wall between them.

That wall consisted of little resentments, the worst kind. Big resentments jerked the angry feelings into words that could be dealt with. Little resentments festered in the darkness of the soul.

At first, Craig's drive and ambition had attracted her. But it was that very earn-till-you-burn attitude that had split them up. They both were busy earning, so their relationship wasn't burning.

She shook her head. "Maybe I need to copy Chad Reese and see a therapist."

Marge scoffed. "Tennis is one of the best therapies available—and cheaper."

"So why aren't you playing tennis?" she challenged.

Her co-worker grinned, looking for all the world like the Cheshire Cat. "Because lovemaking is the other."

"I don't know, Marge. There were times when the sex was good with Craig. Maybe a few times, very few, when it was even great." But never that ultimate connection of the emotional, physical, mental, and spiritual. That wall-socket sex, as Joe had called it.

Marge took a long reflective drag on her cigarette. The haze of smoke filtered out the sprinkling of freckles across her nose. "Maybe you ought to advertise in one of those personals columns. Then you'd be more likely to get what best fits your personality."

"Thirty-four, bright, active, and independent. Seeking male of similar . . ." She scratched through that and started again. "DWF, over thirty, tired of the corporate merry-go-round. Forget lifestyle. Wants life. Loves intellect, humor, and compassion. Seeks soul mate to set out on higher consciousness quest with her."

Keep it simple, baby.

Chapter Three

"My wife died three years ago, and I haven't been able to find anyone I could really talk to. A friend suggested I try the personal columns."

Sarah cradled the receiver between her cheek and shoulder and marked a check beside Douglas's name, one of twenty-three responses she had received to her ad.

"Same here. About the friend's suggestion, that is. Two years ago I broke up with my boyfriend. The interval has been one of real growth, but I have to say that putting the ad in the personals column has been the ultimate in growth experiences."

"I'd like to get to know you better. Would you be available, say midweek, for a cup of coffee?"

*   *   *

"To have an ice-cold beer right now would be to die for, and I don't even like beer." Eyes closed against the bone-leaching sunlight, Sarah sighed and wiped the sweat from her forehead with the back of her hand.

The early April afternoon was unseasonably hot, a withering ninety-three degrees that would have fried a tortilla on the tennis court's asphalt. The water she had brought in her thermos was tepid. Between sets, she and Joe shared a net post that offered about as much shade as a toothpick.

"So, how's the Lonely Hearts column going?"

She watched him tip her thermos to his mouth. Water trickled down his chin and along the muscled column of his throat to collect in blond, curling hair just below. "Rough sailing. One man I had lunch with believed that no one should have a drink before the noon hour, at which time he promptly ordered a Salty Dog. And then another one—and another."

He slid her a sideways grin. "Was he the best of your catch or the worst?"

She grimaced. "I didn't catch anyone. The closest I came to landing a catch was a man by the name of Douglas, who was a widower. Over coffee, he pulled out pictures of his wife. His billfold resembled an album. I wouldn't have been surprised if he had told me he kept a shrine dedicated to her in his bedroom. Honestly, Joe, I felt sympathy for him, but he's no more ready to date than I am. Neither of us should be out there hustling."

"This is a learned art. One has to practice it. You can't rely on hitting a homer your first time at plate, Sarah. Stick with it. The going gets easier."

She rose to her feet and dropped a tennis ball onto his lap. "Easy for you to say. You've been at plate six years now. What do you know about commitment to one person? We've been playing tennis all this time, and you've never discussed your dating life. I think you're a will-o'-the-wisp."

He stared up at her through eyes narrowed against the murderous sunlight. Sweat glistened above the well-defined line of his upper lip. "Why do you say that?"

"You said it yourself. Your freedom is the most important thing to you. The freedom to do what you want, when you want."

He took the balls and sprang to his feet to stare her down. "Freedom isn't everything. Sometimes it's just a mask for my fear."

"You, afraid? You always seem fearless to me. Anyone who gives their spare time to work with our church's cancer and AIDS patients has to be extremely brave."

"It's my way of making myself face my fears. When you confront your fears they can't catch you from behind."

"What are you afraid of?"

"What everyone is afraid of—being vulnerable, getting hurt."

"Yeah," she said softly. "Maybe that's my problem. Maybe, subconsciously, I'm finding excuses not to pursue relationships further with the men I've met. Maybe I haven't given any of them a chance."

When Rhys Jorgenson, a building contractor, responded to her ad, she tried to keep an open mind. "An afternoon sailing on the lake? I'd love it."

Just in case she didn't like it, or him, she agreed to meet him at the lake's docks, where he kept his sailboat. With her own car, flight would be easy.

April 17—When I saw Rhys Jorgenson, my heart did a double take. He sat on the boat deck, one arm propped on a jeaned knee. His face was tanned and his eyes, gray as Norwegian fjords, were bold.

His sailboat was a twenty-six-foot motor model that might as well have been a floating bordello. I could have handled seduction. Rhys wanted more. He wanted challenges. Here was someone intelligent, attractive, with a sense of humor. And challenges made him tick, he said!

Any lucid replies I had hoped to make vanished. When Rhys suggested putting back into port after only two hours on the lake, I felt really low, like I wasn't enough of a woman to captivate his interest. I really feel like abandoning the dating scene altogether.

"So how is love in the personals column? Any prospective Lotharios?"

Sarah grimaced at Joe and accepted the glass of ice tea he handed her. "My stint as first mate for my last ad response sunk quicker than the *Titanic*. I'm abandoning ship and the personal ads."

With a furrowed brow, Joe settled into his well-used recliner and propped an ankle over one bare knee. Great legs. He had been working in his carpentry shop behind his house and was dressed in an old T-shirt and white shorts. Yep, great legs.

She watched him light his pipe. Both its cherry scent and the eddying smoke soothed her. Smoke, he had said, had the qualities of a woman. Mysterious, shape-shifting, elusive.

"Want to tell me about this last date?" he asked. "Or is the subject too painful?"

She turned an idle eye back to his bookcase and its wide range of titles. Well read, the man was. She was returning a book on poetry she had borrowed. Funny, how comfortable she felt. This was what friendship was all about. Being as comfortable as she imagined Joe's old recliner was.

She sighed and flashed him a mock pout. "I am afraid my Viking had a challenging woman in mind."

"And he didn't think you measured up to that ideal? Or you didn't think you did?"

Her fingers ran over the beautifully carved scroll of the bookcase. A sample of Joe's quality work. From the little he said, she gathered that he made nearly as much money from his woodwork as he did as a professor at the local university, which, she understood, wasn't that much. Certainly, his middle-class neighborhood and battered old van reflected his moderate income.

"I didn't think I measured up," she murmured. Her ego still suffered.

"What makes you think that, Sarah?"

She turned from the bookcase to find him watching her, a reflective expression in those sea-calm eyes. Sunlight streamed through the bay window, warming her.

She looked away, letting her gaze travel over his study, messy in a masculine way but not dirty. Her mom would have said, "Clutter alert!"

"I know enough not to try to fool myself, Joe. I don't think I am sensuous or seductive. I consider myself a basic woman, and not a particularly challenging one."

"You love the challenge of a difficult legal case, don't you?"

"Why, yes."

"Well, we all have many sides. We each have a sexual side, as well, but it usually responds in situations where the energies are flowing. Your energies and those of this love pirate simply weren't on the same wave length."

"Oh, stop smirking." But she felt better.

"Mom, were you ever bored with Dad?"

Her mother glanced up from the crossword

puzzle she was working and peered at her from over her thick glasses. "Bored? Angry, maybe. Out of patience. Frustrated. Not even loving him, sometimes. But bored, land's sake no, Sarah."

Sarah rested her head against the back of the overstuffed chair, its blue chintz faded and worn after nearly half a century of use. Had Craig simply grown bored with her?

What worried her even more, had she grown bored with him without even realizing it? Had she just wanted someone, anyone, so much that she would have settled for anything? For someone with whom she had so very little in common?

She still had six briefs to review before bedtime. Wearily, she rose and crossed to the kitchen table, where her mother's pen scratched answers. "You ready for me to take you grocery shopping, Mom?"

Her mother looked up. Concern wrinkled a face already older than its years. "Don't give away your heart to someone who might break it, Sarah."

She felt like grieving for her mother's own hurt. "Mom, what should I wait for? A sign from heaven that here is the man for me? You have to take chances."

Her mother glanced away, as if embarrassed. "I just don't want you to get hurt anymore."

Sarah sighed. "Look, Mom, I won't take any chances unless it's written in the stars, all right?"

Her mother pushed her stooped frame up from

the dining-table chair. "I'd rather take a chance on bingo."

Sarah sank to the court's hot asphalt and stretched out prostrate, her eyes squinting against the merciless sunlight. "I can't keep this up, Joe. I'm burning my candle at both ends."

He dropped down cross-legged beside her and uncapped his thermos. "This is a learning process. You'll survive and emerge even stronger from this dating period."

The tinkling sound of water filling the thermos cap restored her sapped energy. She levered herself into a sitting position. "I suppose you're right. I know I don't want to go back to all work and no play again, no matter how disappointing the play has been."

"Disappointing?" he chided, and passed her the water-filled thermos cap. "Haven't you had fun whipping me at tennis?"

She laughed. "Whipping you? I think I'm the one who has taken the drubbing lately. 6-0, 6-0."

He leaned forward, forearms braced on his knees. "Tell me, Sarah, what was it that galvanized you into searching for a personal life?"

She tilted the cap to her lips and felt the cool water flowing down her throat. "When I knew I had become too performance oriented."

"What happened?"

She focused on the crisp, sun-bleached hairs on his forearms, striated with muscles developed from his carpentry. "I don't know for certain if there was any one thing. Craig and I had broken up, I was depressed, confused and very dissatisfied with my life."

"Despite having achieved the salary, status, and trappings of a successful businesswoman?"

"That was just it. And, yes, I do recall now an incident that triggered my decision to change my lifestyle. After all this time, I had forgotten it.

"I was rushing to Mother's house at lunchtime. She had a doctor's appointment and can't drive, and I was chauffeuring her. I knew I had to hurry back to work, that I had a meeting with an important client, so eating lunch was going to be out of the question.

"Anyway, after I dropped my mother off at her house, I got snarled in traffic. For over an hour, a turtle could have outpaced my car. All I could think of was the chaos that would be awaiting me at the office. Next thing I knew, I was crying. My forehead was resting on the steering wheel, and I was sobbing my heart out.

"That scared me. That's when I decided I had to make some drastic changes in my life. But I started with simple things. Forcing myself to take time for myself. Attending church, playing tennis with you, visiting an art gallery with Marge, that sort of thing."

"But you're still looking for something?"

She stared back into those deep blue eyes. Their

openness gave her the courage to be honest. "I'm ready for the drastic now, Joe. I want to find my soul mate. I want a relationship where we are both totally absorbed in the other, at least until something even finer is created between us."

She waited for some kind of admonishment from him but none came. "I've never experienced it, Sarah, but I believe it exists. That kind of relationship where if you are not looking at each other, you are, at least, looking in the same direction. Just don't ever give up on your dream. Keep looking."

"I tell you there's nothing to it, Sarah. Just make small talk."

Sarah darted a disgusted expression at Marge. They were walking down the dimly lit entrance hall of a Mexican restaurant, where they had agreed to meet Marge's latest dating mate and a friend of his—Sarah's blind date for the evening.

She clutched her purse more tightly against her side. "Small talk I can make. It's the scintillating talk that comes hard for me."

At that hour, the restaurant was virtually empty. She and Marge had come directly from work and were wearing their professional look: Marge in a gray worsted, two-piece suit and red silk blouse; she in a navy-blue, two-piece suit and white shell.

In a far corner, two men sat, smoking. Both rose

at their approach. Tab, Marge's date, put his arm around her waist and gave her a squeeze.

Sarah slid a glance at the other man. He was tall and stocky. His broad face was as tense as she imagined hers must be.

"Tab," Marge said, "I want you to meet my friend, Sarah. Sarah Logan, Tab Brannigan."

Tab was on the portly side but with features as warm as fresh-baked chocolate chip cookies. "Nice to meet you, at last," he said. "Marge has extolled your virtues. This is my friend, Darrin Hedrick, a golf partner of mine."

Darrin shook her hand. Though his grasp was firm enough, his tentative smile betrayed shyness. This appealed to her. "Hi," he said.

Drinks were ordered. Then everyone began to talk at once and next began laughing. "All right," Marge said, "you first, Darrin. Tab tells me you just got back from Russia. What was it like?"

He laughed a little but under Marge's friendly questioning began talking enthusiastically about his business trip to the port of St. Petersburg. His broad face widened even more with his smile. "With the Eastern bloc opening up, our pump sales have skyrocketed."

"Pumps?" This was Marge.

"Yes, my company manufactures seamless pumps for toxic chemicals."

"Then you're making our environment safe?" This was Marge.

"Safe?" Tab chimed in. "Darrin's product is not

only safe but so squeaky clean that it could pump milk to grade schools."

"So Russia's oil industry has to be interested in your product." This was Marge.

Sarah felt like a wilting flower. Why couldn't she be charming and effervescent like Marge?

"It's all in the cards," Marge said. They sat in the firm's dining room. Sarah knew she should be skipping lunch. On her desk was a Mount Everest of notes, waiting to be collated into a trust she was preparing.

Sarah tossed her soda can in the trash. "My clamming up last night with Tab and Darrin was all in the cards?"

"Sure." Marge took a drag on her cigarette. "My astrologist told me this month I would be a magnificent conversationalist."

"Humph! All of that is merely the power of suggestion."

Marge shrugged. "Could be. But having your scope charted can be fun. Why don't you try it?"

April 30—Marge suggested I see an astrologist. I'd rather see Chad Reese's therapist. I'm not that desperate. Yet. I believe my soul mate is seeking me, even as I seek him.

"Your ad really interested me. No come-ons, just openness combined with the willingness to explore and grow."

Over the telephone, Sarah listened to Barry Meniken. He said he had never been married and apparently earned a good income as a painter, if the Lexus he was telling her about actually operated.

She had told Joe she was giving up on the ads, but here she was, interviewing a prospective date. "You mentioned you are taking yoga classes?" she asked.

"T'ai chi. I am trying to center myself more. I believe that if I can isolate myself and focus my thoughts it will give my paintings more depth and expression."

"I understand that total devotion, Barry. When I am focused on my work, nothing else intrudes into my awareness."

Well, that wasn't entirely true. Lately, a vague sort of dissatisfaction was intruding even into her working hours.

"And do you get irritated when other people make demands on your time?" the husky voice at the other end of the telephone line asked.

"Only if it's when I am on a deadline."

"But that should be always! To be true to yourself, your whole life should be devoted to your gift, whether it's painting or practicing law."

She was intrigued by his intensity. "A life like what you describe would be wonderful, but I'm not quite sure what my gift is."

"Well, it's high time you concentrated on discovering your desires, no?"

Yes, she thought, *it is.*

"I know you're not asking my advice, Sarah, but I don't think this Barry is the right man for you."

The gorgeous Sunday morning sunshine suddenly became hazy as a sliver of a cloud passed over. "I don't know how you can say that, Joe."

He set his coffee cup on a marble table. "Did he mention children? Pets? Friends? A man who is centered totally on his work is centered on himself."

She sipped her coffee thoughtfully, her gaze fastened unseeingly on the maze of holly that laced the church's courtyard. Smokers and, on pretty days, other church members slipped out here between services. "Is that so wrong—to focus your attention on something you love, like your painting? Or your books. Or your carpentry?"

"To focus your attention or *all* your attention all the time? People who do that are often children themselves. They want all the attention." Slashes of dimples bracketed his mouth with a dry smile. "They may resent it when someone at the next table is choking to death."

She flashed him a disgusted look. "Barry doesn't seem that insensitive."

Joe downed the last of his coffee, then said, "Maybe not, but I'm just advising you to keep an open mind on this date, before you go falling head over heels in love with this guy."

* * *

May 15—Should have listened to Joe. Thank God, he's not one of those I-told-you-so people. The picnic outing with Barry, the painter, was, to say the least, a memorable one. His profile was that of a Nordic warrior, powerful even in repose. Yet his artistic sensitivity kept that masculinity from crossing the demarcation into the macho syndrome. All I could think of was, yes, this is the man I've been searching for.

On the way up the mountain, we discussed relationships. He believes a man and a woman should be wholly committed to one another if the relationship is to succeed.

I thought so, too. Guess I was wrong.

After we spread the blanket in a periwinkle clearing and divided the deli veggies, he proceeded to expand on his relationship theory that a man and his love mate should isolate themselves from the contamination of society. Go up in the mountains and live as one with nature.

My argument that isolation limited growth was countered by the statement that isolation excluded any interference in the growth of a relationship.

I really wanted to understand this man, because I felt that with him could come a combustion strong enough to explode a chemistry lab. But Joe's words of caution kept me from being totally open to Barry's free ideas.

By the time Barry was explaining that because his father's career as a State Supreme Court judge and his mother's as city manager had bonded them together "so that no one else existed," I knew that not even Barry had existed. As Joe had warned, Barry was the little boy craving all the attention.

Damn it, Joe planted seeds of doubt and ruined my garden of pleasure!

Chapter Four

Sarah sat at her apartment desk and leafed through the draft of the motion she had prepared yesterday. Occasionally, she made a notation in the margin. There were too many errors that could cost her client the case—and cost her a senior partnership. But did she really want that?

Damn it, my mind isn't on my work. I used to love the challenging intricacies of motions and petitions and appeals. Now I'm simply bored.

When she spotted another loophole she had left, she slammed her pencil down with a muttered curse. The pencil cracked. Wood splinters drove into her palm. A whimper of pain escaped her at the same time her apartment doorbell rang.

"Damn!" she said again, her eyes smarting with tears.

When she opened the door, Joe stood there, his arms ladened with a stack of books. "Just returning what I borrowed, before you charge me for being overdue . . . Sarah, you've been crying?"

With a grimace, she held up her hand. A few faint red streaks told the reason for her distress. "I broke a pencil, and it jabbed into my palm." She stepped back for him to enter.

He set the books on her entryway chest. "Let me see your hand."

She surrendered her palm to his examining fingers. "Hmmm, nothing broken."

She winced when his probing search touched her forefinger. "Yes, there is. My heart."

From beneath those curling blond lashes, he studied her face. "Your heart is broken?"

She nodded and turned away, walking barefoot into the narrow little kitchen. Joe followed. He was dressed for tennis. She had forgotten they had discussed a Saturday match.

Any other man and she would have been embarrassed at her dishabille. On Saturday mornings, she refused to dress. But Joe was like an old friend. She didn't mind him catching her in her rather flimsy nightgown.

"Don't say you warned me." She picked up her cup and tossed the stale coffee down the sink. "Want a cup of coffee?"

"The artist?"

"Don't smirk." She poured herself a cup and turned back to him. "You know, I detest people like you who rise early on Saturday mornings with a smile on their faces and a song in their hearts."

He took her cup from her and took a swallow of the coffee. "Just a sip of yours. Caffeine's bad for me." His grin was mischievous. "At my age, one has to—"

She snorted. "Your age. You're just a youngster, Joe."

He passed the cup back to her. "So are you. You're just determined to act like you're older. I think we're the same age, spirit-wise. Isn't it just possible you could be an old soul in a young body?"

She wasn't sure if he was joking. "Joe, I once mentioned I was searching for my soul mate. Do you believe in . . ." She felt silly but went ahead, " . . . in them, in soul mates?"

"Certainly."

"You do?"

He leaned back against the counter. "Sometimes, though, we fail to recognize our soul mate."

"Yeah, like ships passing in the night. An opportunity that knocks only—"

"Oh, no. I don't believe we get only one chance at uniting with our soul mate." He crossed his feet at his ankles and folded his arms. Her gaze fell on their curling blond hair. "If we don't match up in this lifetime, then the next or the next."

"Or even a previous one, huh?"

"Oh, yes," he said with enthusiasm. "Someone you have loved in the past, love in this lifetime, and will love again. I have this theory that the same groups of people travel together through eternity just in different roles." He shrugged those massive shoulders. "Who knows, Sarah? No one. So my theory is as good as anyone else's, right?"

His tone indicated that he was about to dismiss the subject, but she was intrigued. "How would you recognize your soul mate?"

He thought for a moment. "Well, for one, I'd say that you should look for the kind of relationship that grows better and stronger with time. That weathers the storms. That reveals the best part of ourselves."

"I know," she mused. "A best friend yet lover who understands our deepest yearnings." Now she was getting carried away, too. "When you are united with the person you alone are meant for, some other outside force, something greater than two single individuals, is created."

"But that interacting love can only come about by loving unconditionally. By casting out all doubts and fears of being hurt."

"In spite of the things the other person does that drives you batty, you still have that sense of oneness. As if you were one being, but for some reason you had to part so you could better appreciate each other before you came together again."

His smile showed uneven, but beautifully white teeth. Craig's had been perfect, perfectly capped, that was. "I think you got the idea, Logan. Now get your butt in gear and get dressed, or we'll lose our court."

She set down her cup and flashed him a look of mock anger. "Don't you ever think about anything besides carpentry and tennis?"

As she turned to leave the kitchen, he said, "Hey, Logan."

She looked over her shoulder. "Yeah?"

That warmly wise smile again. "Your heart will survive the artist to love again."

May 18—Are we watching the same bright star, Soul Mate? Are you wishing and waiting, just like me? Waiting. Waiting.

"There really aren't any males in my life right now. Not even a tomcat," Sarah told the astrologist Marge had recommended.

This was just a waste of money. But it *was* something different. It added a touch of spice to the endless calendar of days. Of rising, going to work, coming home, going to bed.

"Well, that is if you don't count the man I play tennis with once a week," she amended.

The heavy-set, baggy-eyed man glanced at her charts full of scribbled hieroglyphics spread before him. "Hmmm. What is his birth date?"

"His birth date?" She had been playing tennis with Joe for almost half a year now. Surely, he had mentioned his birth date. She knew she was about ten years younger than he. "Oh, yeah, December

27, 1947." The day before her dad's birth date.

The astrologist consulted a tome, some kind of planetary guide. "Hmmmm."

"What is it?" Maybe Joe was born in the year for axe murderers.

The astrologist rubbed the more prominent of his chins. "Interesting. The man's birth date signifies that he could be an extremely liberating sexual partner."

She almost choked. Joe, a sexual partner? "What else?"

"The energies present at his birth date tell me that his planetary energies in conjunction with someone who has a planetary arrangement like yours could result in a very uninhibited sensual experience."

June 17—I don't want a liberating sexual experience. I want a soul mate!

"What do you think you do best?" Joe asked.

He and Sarah sat in a submarine sandwich shop and drank ice tea from plastic cups. Although the air conditioning was blasting, sweat generated by two sets of tennis beaded on their faces. Her hair, clasped at her nape, was wringing wet.

She flashed him a sly grin. "I can give you a good drubbing in tennis."

He settled back in the restaurant chair and lit his pipe. She reflected that watching him smoke the pipe was soothing to her. He never seemed to hurry and hustle. Except on the court. "Seriously, Sarah."

"Oh, I don't know." Proclaiming her good points had always been difficult for her. "I believe I have been a good attorney."

"What else?"

"Well, I'm a good listener. I think I am resilient. A care-giver. Reasonably intelligent. There, now what about you?"

"You didn't mention something I think you're very good at."

"What's that?"

"You're fun."

"I am?"

"And you're cute. I know you think you're too serious to be cute, but you're not."

At a loss for words, she stared at her hands cupped around her plastic glass and realized that her arms and wrists and hands were taking on a darker, rosier color. Could she actually be blushing? Or was it just the heat bringing a flush to her skin?

She mustered a steady voice. "And you? What do you do best?"

A wry grin deepened his dimples. "I can only go by what some women have told me—that I am an extremely passionate man."

Her attention was jerked to the forefront! Was this a come-on?

She studied him from beneath her lashes. No, Joe had not made the statement as a suggestive innuendo. He had never been one for that. He had never come on to her in all the time they had been playing tennis. He was just stating a fact.

She braved a question. "Passionate about life or about love?"

"Both. But then solitary confinement would make someone that way. You end up appreciating the warmth of the sun and the texture of human skin."

That night she lay awake, thinking about what Joe had said, about what the astrologist had said in regard to Joe's birth date and planetary arrangements, and about those empty years of her own lackluster sex life. Less than fulfilling.

She found it difficult to get to sleep. In fact, she found it difficult thinking about anything else over the days that followed. So much so that she wasted half a day preparing a case argument that wasn't even on the docket yet. She just couldn't keep her mind on priorities.

The next Wednesday couldn't come quickly enough. Across the net from Joe, she stared at him with eyes narrowed skeptically. Sexy? Not in her wildest dreams! Less than average height, balding, middle-aged.

But then, she was no Aphrodite. However, she did possess a desire for sexual passion—that union of man and woman that could eclipse all other feelings. She knew sexual passion existed. She had just never experienced it.

"Hey, pay attention, Logan," Joe called. "When I can serve you up an ace, then I know you're out in left field."

She decided to experiment. "I wasn't ready." She walked to the back court. She leaned forward in a receiving position, racket between both hands, and gently swayed her hips from side to side.

Nothing. Except she lost the point.

"Hey, Logan, are you staying out too late nights on these dates? You're dragging around the court like a limp noodle."

She tried again, this time with a little more tail action. Again nothing.

Subtlety didn't work. Blatant action was needed.

At the next change of sides, she halted at the net and said, "I visited an astrologist." She half expected him to make fun of her. But he surprised her.

"Did you now?" Those golden-fringed eyes studied her face. "And did he tell you that your soul mate was written in the stars?"

She toyed with her racket strings. "I did it on a lark. And I thought why not carry it through on a lark, just to see."

"Carry what through?"

"The astrologist told me you could be my great, liberating sexual experience."

She glanced up at him, waiting. He tilted his head. Sunlight glistened on his suntanned skin.

He continued to study her though those pale curly lashes. Perspiration ran down her rib cage. "Well, will you?" she asked, impatient and feeling more like a fool than ever before.

"Will I what?"

"Will you make love to me?"

Another long silence. She could hear the cicada mocking her request.

He looked out through the wire fence at something that probably only he could see. "This isn't something we would do in the back seat of the car or at your place. There are too many distractions—chores you think you should be doing, the telephone. This requires a special place."

"I just don't want . . . well, one of those motels with paper-thin walls."

"That's not what I had in mind, Sarah."

"My—my request doesn't surprise you."

"No, you have always been unusual." He smiled. "At least, I have always thought so. I think a Fantasy Island weekend would fulfill what we both have in mind. How about in three weeks? Could you go away then?"

She nodded dumbly. She hadn't expected a whirlwind to dance through her life like this. Especially not a whirlwind that came in the form of laid-back, laconical Joe Smith.

Each Wednesday for the next three weeks, they played tennis. Sometimes they talked about the upcoming weekend getaway. "I have reservations at Reefer's Point in Bristol Cay," he said, when they were both at the net. "A four-star resort in the Caribbean."

"Oh, Joe, that sounds lovely!" Guilt assaulted her. Could Joe afford something so luxurious?

"Well, I didn't want your grand seduction of me to take place in some seedy joint," he said with a straight face.

She chuckled, feeling relieved. Joe was a grown man and could take care of his finances without her direction. "I guess I sounded a little melodramatic about thin-walled motels."

A part of her wondered if perhaps, without knowing it, she had seduced Joe. Maybe, unconsciously, she had been seducing him all along. Or perhaps, he had been unconsciously seducing her, also. As if their affair had been fated or something. She shook her head. A ridiculous thought.

She felt silly and a little shy. "I've just never done something like this before."

He grinned. Beautiful white teeth sparkled in the sunlight. His smile transformed his average features into an arresting face. "Neither have I."

On another Wednesday, they discussed ground rules for their weekend affair.

"I want you to understand that after we return from this—from our trip together, that our friendship resumes its normal boundaries," she said, hearing and hating the officious tone of her voice.

Thank God for Joe's humor. "I was about to suggest the same thing. After all, how can I expect to win at tennis if I have to cope with your seductive behavior afterward?"

Her smile ebbed from her face. "Joe, we've always been able to talk about anything. Lately, I've been worried that maybe I somehow had that as an intention all along—to seduce you."

He stopped in the act of tugging a sweat band onto his wrist. "Sarah, for God's sake, don't go analyzing what's between us. That's what's made it so special. Let's just take it as it comes. All right?"

Still, on another Wednesday, as they sat resting between sets, she said, "I know you said not to analyze our relationship, but this is just something I have to ask."

"You ask a lot of questions, Sarah. Always keeping me on my toes, aren't you? Okay, go ahead."

"Why did you agree to—to make love to me?"

He tossed and caught the ball several times in his left hand. "Oh, I think your forthrightness. You didn't try to manipulate me. You just came right out and asked. That appealed to me."

She felt a wave of heat, stealing up her throat. "I tried flirting. You didn't notice."

The ball ceased its air dance. He flicked her a puzzled glance. "When?"

"The Wednesday I asked you to make love to me. I, ummm, tried wriggling my bottom while I was waiting for you to serve."

Realization dawned in his expression. "That was what you were doing? I thought you were trying out a new stance. You know, like the way Martina Navratilova dances on her toes while waiting for a serve."

They both laughed. She marveled how at ease she felt with Joe. Before, she had been unnaturally suspicious of men. She had always worried about what they would demand of her. Undoubtedly, an old tape supplied by her mother, who believed that happiness came at a price.

Well, she was willing to pay that price, to take that chance of suffering pain. To play it safe and avoid pain, meant also avoiding happiness. She could very well end up like her mother, a prisoner of her own fear. A far worse prison than what Joe must have endured.

July 2—In five days I go away for a weekend with Joe. What have we wrought?

Chapter Five

"My highest hope is for a river of passion," Joe said quietly.

Those words struck a chord of desire in Sarah. She turned from the plane's window to search his powerful features. Why had she seen only the roundness of his face and not the sensuality in the set of his mouth and the patrician strength of a nose like the one which Michelangelo had carved into a gladiator sculpture?

She turned from Joe's patient gaze. Why had she never really considered the nobility of the man himself? "I would like that, also. If only I am not afraid."

He took her hand. Incredible, they had yet to kiss even. "Afraid?"

"I don't know . . . afraid of experiencing the full range of my sexuality maybe. This all seems . . . What I have started seems . . . bizarre."

He squeezed her hand. "How about extraordinary? I like that word much better."

She tested the word in her mind. Yes, extraordinary was a better word.

"To be in control of one's emotions, one must first experience no control," he went on. "I learned that during those years of isolation as a political hostage. Once the emotions are free, then they can be contained or expressed at will."

"And that's what I am to learn?" she murmured.

"I don't know, Sarah. Perhaps we'll have a merging of ourselves into one, if only briefly, a communion of our inner selves—if neither of us is afraid."

Never had she suspected the depth of this man, her friend. She rested her head on his shoulder. She felt such peace at that moment.

The peace began to recede the instant the commuter plane touched down on Bristol Cay's runway. Exotic colors clamored for her attention: the bright green of jungle vegetation that encroached on the runway; the endless turquoise ocean hovering just beyond; the black, saffron, toast, and tea-rose skin shades of the people at the small airport, most of them involved in the service-oriented island community as porters, drivers, vendors.

The smiling men and women wore skimpy, light clothing of the most vivid colors. She envied their attire. The muggy heat back home should have prepared her for this climate, but this humid, tropical heat extracted every last ounce of her energy.

A young man with sun-blond hair and a surfer's tan took their luggage and put it in the trunk of his taxi. "Where to?"

"Reefer's Point," Joe said, opening the taxi's back door for her. Its windows were down, which meant no air conditioning. Was this a bad omen for the great sexual awakening she was supposed to experience?

She shuddered.

"You can't be chilled," Joe drawled, concern furrowing his golden brows.

She shook her head. "No. Just apprehensive. I've been anticipating this moment for weeks. Now all this seems too sudden. I'm not sure I can handle it."

"You don't have to handle anything, Sarah." He put his arm around her. "You don't have to do anything. You just have to be. Be yourself. That's all I want from you."

Oh, God, she thought, *such a man seems too good to be true. At long last, will my yearnings be fulfilled?*

The taxi passed through massive gates with a small bronzed plaque declaring Reefer's Point. A winding, bougainvillea-lined drive made a loop

Parris Afton Bonds

before a sprawling white, two-story plantation house.

Joe helped her alight from the taxi. Baroque doorways opened both at the building's front and across the foyer, where a tantalizing view of azure sea beckoned.

Her first impression upon entering the building was its coolness then the sound of crashing surf coming from the ocean side. The registration desk was just past a triple-tiered lava stone fountain. A ceiling fan, reminiscent of the tropical rooms of British colonial India, swished lazily from above.

With nerves stretched as tightly as a tennis racket, Sarah watched Joe check in. Amazing. In a mere matter of minutes, she would be going to bed with this man, who now seemed more stranger than friend. She was being forced to look at him in an entirely different light.

As he strolled back to her, her heart started to beat unnaturally. "Ready?" he asked.

She nodded. Words weren't going to come. Her knees felt weak. What in the hell was she doing? She was ten times more nervous than she had been taking her bar exams. By all rights, at this time in her life, with her maturity and experience, she should be in control.

Wasn't that what Joe had told her? That she needed to lose control?

He took her hand and stared down at her. "Your palm is clammy."

She stepped into the elevator with him and stared straight ahead at the richly paneled doors. "I'm nervous," she said softly.

He took her hand again. "Trust me, Sarah."

She slanted him a sidewise glance. "I wouldn't be here if I didn't."

He released her hand to clasp her shoulders and turn her to him. "I'm asking for full trust from you. Full surrender."

Her breath lodged in her throat. "I don't know what that means."

He smiled gently. "I know. I'll show you."

Her knees turned to marshmallow, weaker than after three sets of strenuous tennis. While he opened the door to their room, she leaned against the wall for support.

"This is better than I had anticipated!" He turned to her. "Milady." He stepped back for her to enter.

She entered, stopping just inside the doorway. An expanse of glass afforded a panorama of sea and sky. Hibiscus spilled over the balcony's wrought-iron railing. Sunlight flooded the suite, done in shades of terra cotta, peach, and avocado. "How absolutely lovely."

"Come on out onto the balcony. I can never get enough of sunlight."

He opened one of the triple set of French doors. Reluctantly, she followed. He stood at the railing, his gaze seeming to take in every object: the dark green mountains; the colonial town of Bristol, its white buildings ringing the harbor like a string of pearls; the tall white lighthouse, standing sentinel over the bay.

"Your freedom is the most important thing in your life, isn't it?"

He looked over at her. "Don't ever take it for granted, Sarah."

"And yet you're asking me to surrender to you?" she whispered.

His eyes held hers in a steady gaze. "Not to me. To us. For this moment. For now. That's all there is . . . only now. Something else invaluable I learned while imprisoned."

The scent of the tropical flowers was heady, overpowering. "Will you kiss me, Joe?" She couldn't bear to climb into the king-sized bed with him without some show of affection first.

She trembled as he approached her. He cupped her face between his hands and lightly kissed her lips. The lingering kiss left her breathless and weak.

When he released her, she stared up at him. "How did that happen?" she asked without thinking, then blushed. "Maybe it was just me."

"No, it was both of us. And it happened because we both want this. Now, let's have lunch and scout out Bristol."

The relief on her face must have been obvious, because he said, "Yeah, me too. We both need time to know each other on an even more intimate basis before consummating our lovemaking."

Lovemaking? Oh, God, what if she wasn't adequate? "Uh, Joe, my experience is sort of . . . limited."

He dropped a kiss on the tip of her nose. "I'm not here because I want to bed a woman skilled in the art. Why don't you put on a pair of shorts or jeans, and we'll tour Bristol by rented Moped."

She hadn't ridden a scooter since she and a high-school date had prankishly ridden his around the stadium track during a football game. "Oh, I'd love it, Joe!"

He prudently remained on the balcony while she did a quick change in the bathroom. Light blue denim cutoffs with a white-and-blue designer T-shirt completed her casual ensemble. While she refreshened her make-up, Joe changed into something cooler—shorts, also. Ah, those great legs of his.

Riding a Moped in a British possession, she discovered, was more difficult than she had expected, and she was glad that she had Joe to follow. "I can't get used to turning into far left lanes," she said, laughing, as she halted her Moped beside his at a stoplight.

He grinned. "I know. I find myself glancing in the wrong direction for oncoming traffic. Well, what's it to be—the alligator farm or the city market?"

She wrinkled her nose. "You have to ask?"

"The city market it is then."

The quaint hand-laid brick streets were narrow and flanked by small buildings of the British colonial style. Most of them had been converted to gift shops or restaurants.

Parking their Mopeds, she and Joe explored the open shops, cooled only by ceiling fans. Floors were covered in chipped floral tiles. The shops' charm lay not in the achievement but in the attempt.

Hand in hand, she and Joe strolled through aisles of imprinted T-shirts, duty-free perfumes, 180-proof Tortuga Rum, and black coral from the reefs just beyond the wave-lapped shores. The clerks were all friendly, responding with Harry Belafonte ease, "Yeah, mon."

Joe propelled her toward a candle shop, where he purchased a dozen red candles of varying size. "Red is for passion," he said, sending her an oblique glance.

She blushed.

"This is what you want, isn't it, Sarah? A weekend of passion?"

"After which, we resume our friendship," she reminded him.

"Naturally."

They continued on their perusal of the shops. One black man extolled the virtues of a dainty, black coral necklace she admired. "It's owner is assured of returning to Bristol one day, mon."

Joe insisted on buying it for her. "Everyone needs assurance of some future escape to paradise."

She heard the wistful tone in his deep voice as she lifted her hair for him to fasten the clasp at her nape. Delicious shudders ran through her at the brush of his fingers.

Just about the time her stomach was protesting in hunger, Joe suggested they eat. Along the harbor, free of the tourist crowds, they found a small restaurant with a courtyard looking out on the bay. Beneath the dappled shade of a secluded baobab tree, they selected a wrought-iron table that gave them a view of cruise ships, freighters, and motorboats plying the bay's placid, azure waters. Faint chords of reggae music drifted from the interior of the restaurant.

After they ordered a late lunch of crab salad, Joe narrowed his gaze on the pristine white buildings lining the bay like a horseshoe. "We take so much for granted. I make it a point to imprint scenes like this one in my memory. To draw upon should I ever again be incapacitated by either my health or circumstances."

Her fingers touched the black coral nestled between her breasts. The nugget would always be a reminder of Joe. "I can't even begin to imagine how horrendous being held hostage must be."

He took a swallow of his chilled sangria. "Your emotions are on a roller coaster. Fear that you'll never be released, anger that this could happen to you and no one does anything to help, apathy, the overwhelming desire to die and get the waiting, the life-long waiting, over."

She traced the glass rim of her ruby-red drink. "You must be very bitter about losing three years of your life."

He turned those intuitive blue eyes on her. "Never. No one can afford bitterness."

"I'm just now learning that," she said, thinking of her mother's bitterness.

His mouth curved in a knowing smile. "As a matter of fact, Sarah, I am grateful. I would have gone through life never appreciating what is really important. Not money or power, but people . . . and the moment. I learned to forget the past and not anticipate the future."

This was what she needed to learn for herself. Despite the wisdom of his words, she couldn't help but anticipate with some anxiety the evening— and the rest of the weekend. What had she gotten herself into?

He reached across the table and put his hand over hers. "Stop worrying about tonight."

"You even read my mind?" She hoped she sounded lighthearted.

He gave her a wry grin. "No, I'm reading mine. I imagine you must be thinking the same thing."

"Which is?"

"Which is concern about ruining a good friendship."

"Well, don't worry about me ruining things by falling in love with you. I won't."

His mouth formed a twisted smile. "Thanks." He tugged on her hand. "Come on. Let's go dancing."

"Like this?" She glanced down at her shorts.

"Hey, mon," he said, imitating the local patois, "somebody gotta do it." He winked at her. "Besides, no one dresses formal here, don't you know?"

With the sun casting rays of red across the sea, they returned to their hotel. Arm and arm, they walked through the lobby toward the nightclub entrance. Inside, one wall of floor-to-ceiling glass gave a view of the free-form pool, fed by a waterfall. Low-growing tropical plants spilled over its lava rock rim. The same soft lights that lit the nightclub glowed around the pool.

A five-piece band played romantic music to which a dozen or so couples were dancing. To Sarah's relief, most of them were as casually dressed as she and Joe. After they ordered drinks at a table looking out over the pool, he asked her to dance. "All day, I've been wanting to hold you."

On the dance floor, she moved easily to his lead. He was the perfect height for her. She could hear his breath rustling at her ear. "Why haven't you? Held me, I mean. Held me before this even?"

He drew back so that he could see her face. "Don't you know that I get nervous, too?"

"With me?"

73

"Of course. I want everything to go right for you. You're a very intense person, you know. You deserve to feel you're worthy of intense attention. Focused devotion and total passion."

His words stunned her. In her heart of hearts, she hadn't really taken the astrologist's message seriously. Was this one of those self-fulfilling prophecy things?

She nuzzled her cheek against his. The faint scent of his cologne teased her nose. His jaw was shadowed with stubble that lightly rasped the tender skin at her temple, a pleasant remind-er of the differences in their sexes and how they complemented one another.

They danced several more slow songs and fin-ished their drinks before a look passed between them.

He dropped several folded bills on the table and took her hand. "We've waited long enough, Sarah."

On the way to their room, a part of her acknowl-edged that this was undoubtedly the most roman-tic episode of her entire life!

Another part of her fretted about those most intimate of moments that were soon to come. Once she and Joe reached their suite, he began to take the candles from their shopping bags.

She stood rooted just inside the room, feeling like Lot's wife, turned to a pillar of salt.

He paused in lighting a candle and looked up at her. "I'll order wine in a moment."

"I can do that." She had to do something in order to exert her need for control.

"Great," he said, lighting the last candle. "I'd like to take a quick shower."

By the time she ordered wine and hor d'oeuvres, Joe had finished showering. He came out of the tiled bathroom wearing only jeans and a towel around his neck. She had never realized what a broad chest he had. And all that blond hair curling around his small nipples!

Her shower was even quicker. She changed into a slinky hostess gown of apricot silk that swished around her legs.

When she left the steamy bathroom, low music from the radio was playing. Candles reflected in the suite's mirrors, hundreds of star points of light. The scents of the myriad flowers spilling over the balcony floated in through the open French doors.

"You truly are beautiful, Sarah," Joe said.

She didn't know how to handle this aspect of her relationship with Joe, so she said flippantly, "That's not what a friend would say."

"It's exactly what a friend would say."

She started to object but said instead, "I think I miss our old . . . camaraderie."

He smiled and took her hands to draw her to him. "It still exists. It's just that another element has been added."

"And that is?"

His broad forehead furrowed. "I'm not sure yet the range of our broadened friendship, but I do

·know this. Only good can come of it."

She didn't know how to accept what he was telling her.

He lowered his head slightly. She waited, expecting him to kiss her, but instead he left their hands at their sides, their palms touching lightly. She kept her eyes on his and let him stare into her eyes and her soul. She was open and vulnerable.

He whispered, "Breathe in and out slowly, your lips closed, Sarah."

She did as he told her. Soon, she realized she was matching her breath to his.

"When our breathing is harmonious," he told her, "we know that the two of us are capable of forging a deep connection."

Indeed, a pleasant tingling began in her palms, where they touched his, then traveled up her arms to radiate throughout her body.

Lightly, leisurely, he began to touch her. She was surprised how right it felt. He stroked the full length of her arms, lifting her hair to let it cascade again around her shoulders.

The kiss, coming at last, was something wondrous. Her attorney's sharp mind faded. For once in her life, she forgot to think, to analyze. She just felt . . . felt out of her body, as if floating, felt separate but one with this marvelous man.

Somehow, she knew she was sinking to the floor, stretching out on the lush carpet with the candlelight dancing all around her and Joe.

Somehow, he had shed his jeans. And somehow, she was aroused as she had never been before.

He began undoing the tie at her waist. As the silky material fell away, her hands quickly covered her exposed breasts. Gently, he took hold of her wrists and moved her hands. "You're beautiful to me."

"I'm far from perfect, Joe."

With a reproving smile, he shook his head. "I don't want some model-thin woman with breasts like dried raisins and vinegar running through her veins. The media has surrounded us with perfect bodies, but they have no reality." He cupped her chin and kissed her lips ever so softly. "Besides, what is being in love but a state of mind?"

"This is too much to think about at once," she murmured. Her head lolled to one side and her lids drifted closed, as she savored the feeling of his fingers exploring her body—the indentations of her waist, the curve of her breasts, the column of her neck. She trembled at the delicious feelings.

"Don't think, Sarah. Just surrender."

The part of her she had always held back, she now gave completely. As Joe moved over her, she gazed up into his face and watched without flinching while his eyes lovingly traveled over her body revealed in all its imperfections—and in all its glory and uniqueness.

In his expression, she read her own thought—marveling that they had both overlooked the other's beauty. Her gaze traveled over his body, so definitely male. Her fingers tentatively touched the crisp, golden hair, curling just below his navel. His gasp pleased her.

When he lowered himself and entered her, she was momentarily surprised at her wetness. Her body had responded without any preliminary preparation but her mind had totally focused on something, someone, other than herself.

He began a rhythmical thrusting, and her hands clutched his muscled upper arms in sudden fear. If she gave in to this stranger, she would have nothing of herself left. "Joe," she gasped, "I don't think I'm . . ."

He stopped, rested on his forearms, and stared down at her with heat-glazed eyes. "Hush, Sarah. You're using words as a wall, as a defense. You're creating separation."

"What do you mean?"

"Emotionally." With a wise smile, he pushed the hair back from her face. "If we're to achieve this sexual ecstasy your astrologist foretold, then we've got to be as one—in all ways."

He glanced over at the digital clock. "Fifteen minutes. For fifteen minutes I want you to be silent. Stop talking, stop thinking. Just feel. All right?"

She moved as one with him. Something in her was building. Together, they were creating something grander than the two of them separate. She began quivering uncontrollably. Were those her little mews of pleasure?

When she felt the orgasm coming, she wasn't surprised. It was what followed that was totally unexpected. She went beyond orgasm, reaching that magical feeling of . . . yes, that feeling of ecstasy. Sexual ecstasy. It was a transcendent experience of her mind and body and spirit.

Without knowing why, she burst into tears.

Above her, Joe smiled tenderly and stroked her tear-dampened tendrils from her cheek. "Just think. Our weekend is only beginning."

And too soon would be ended, to return to the friendship of before, she thought with an inexplicable sadness.

Chapter Six

August 3—At last, at long last, I've found my soul mate.

Sarah put down her pen and leafed back through her journal. Amazing. All those entries that recorded her longing for her soul mate. And Joe had been there all along, right under her nose!

True, he hadn't met her expectations of what a perfect soul mate should be. Even though she hadn't wanted a man driven by the need to succeed, she had wanted someone who could offer her a little of life's luxuries. Something that Joe couldn't afford to do.

Could she resolve these conflicting needs? And what were Joe's feelings about their relationship now?

* * *

"Well?" Marge asked. "What happened?"

Sarah swallowed a bite of her baked potato. The office microwave served up cardboard food. The extended weekend trip with Joe had put her behind schedule at work, and lunch at her desk was in order. "Oh, we went shopping in the market, snorkeling, walking along the beach at moonlight. That sort of thing."

"You know that's not what I mean."

"I don't know how to answer your question."

Marge settled back into the chair opposite Sarah's desk and took another puff of her cigarette. "I guess I am being too probing?"

She managed a smile. "I couldn't produce a better answer, Marge, if Racehorse Haynes himself were interrogating me."

In truth, she felt protective about what had transpired between her and Joe over the long, wonderful weekend.

"Come on, we're not talking interrogation. We're talking passion."

"All I can say is that it was something mystical, magical." It was even more than that. She felt bemused. Dazed.

"Monday mornings have a way of bursting balloons," Marge drawled. "So hold on to yours. Don't let Mondays—or me—burst your happiness. You deserve it." She stubbed out her cigarette in a ceramic ashtray. "Just overlook my nosy curiosity. I was out of line."

As the days went by, Sarah's euphoria-filled balloon began to leak. Joe did not call. She did not know why she expected him to do so. Had they not agreed everything would return to their prior status after the weekend?

By the time Wednesday afternoon came around, she was strung out. When the doorbell rang, her heart thudded in her ears loudly. She took a moment to clear her throat and put on a cheery smile before answering the door.

Joe had never looked so attractive, especially with that new Caribbean tan. "Hi," she said. She felt like a sixteen-year-old schoolgirl.

"Hi." He tucked his hands in his shorts pockets. "I've missed you."

"I've missed you, too."

"Well, we'd better hustle if we're going to get a court."

"Yeah."

The day was sunny and gorgeous. And everything felt wrong. She was tongue-tied. She was awkward in her ground strokes. She felt ill at ease with Joe.

When she ran to the net to field a short shot, she stopped short—and started crying. She dropped the racket and covered her face with her hands. Her humiliation was unbearable.

"Sarah, what is it?"

When she got control of herself, she looked at him. The net separated them. He appeared as distraught as she. "It's not working, is it? Our friendship. We've ruined it. Our lifestyles are too opposite."

"Complementary could be a better word."

"We can't go back, can we? Ever?"

She had been hoping he would tell her she was wrong, but he shook his head. "No, we can't." He leaned across the net and picked up her racket. "I'll take you home, Sarah."

August 14—Six months from Valentine's Day and that first tennis date with Joe. Maybe there really isn't such a thing as a soul mate. At least a soul mate for me. Not in this lifetime, anyway.

The next few days were desolate ones. She didn't know whether to hope she would run into Joe at church on Sunday or dread the possibility. What was left to say to one another? She had been foolish to risk certain friendship for a mere chance at feeling ecstasy.

Saturday morning, she sat at her desk, playing catch up on her office work. She realized that all these years she had been losing out by not being with the people who were so important in her life. How long would they be there for her while she tried to find time for them?

She thought about the small resentments she felt when she had to take time from work to chauffeur her mother. And the times when she had been too busy for Craig. And he for her.

The telephone rang, bringing her back from her reverie and reminding her that she still had hours of work left. Irritated, she grabbed the receiver. "Hello?"

"Ms. Logan? Sarah Logan?"

"Yes? This is she."

"This is Friendsbrook General Hospital. We don't know what happened, but your mother was found on her sidewalk by a neighbor and brought her by ambulance. Your mother's vitals are stable at the present, but we'd like you to come in."

Sarah's heart knocked against her rib cage. "I'll be right there."

She took only time enough to throw on a rumpled pair of jeans, shirt, and shoes. *Oh God, don't let Mom die.* She thought of all the things she should have said and hadn't like "I love you, Mom. Just like you are, grumpiness and all."

The ICU room was a nightmare of practicality yet insensitivity. Everywhere monitors recorded her mother's vitals, heart, intake, output. Several IVs and a catheter swung like macabre Mayday streamers from her sheet-shrouded body.

"Hello, Mom," she said softly and touched her mother's papery flesh.

The old woman's lids fluttered.

Sarah leaned over, kissed her cheek, and whispered, "Hang in there. The Eastern Star home is starting up its bingo games."

Her mother's voice struggled to speak, raspy sounds. Sarah leaned closer. "Fie on bingo, Sarah.

85

The stars . . . It's written in the stars!"

"What, Mom?" Panic filled her. Had the stroke affected her mother's mind?

Was that a wink her mother made? "Pay . . . attention to the stars, Sarah."

"Good evening, Sarah."

She glanced around and saw Orville Harrison, their family doctor. To her he had always seemed as old as Methuselah and as wise as Solomon. She beckoned him outside the room. "How is Mom, Dr. Harrison?"

He sat down on the cracked, naugahyde-covered couch in the hallway and clasped his hands between his legs. He looked tired. "We believe she has had a cerebral hemorrhage."

"How bad is it?"

He glanced down at his clasped veined hands and then directed an ironic smile at her. "It's all in God's hands. We'll know more in seventy-two hours, but I think her chances are good."

For the next twenty-four hours, Sarah stayed at her mother's side, but her thoughts roamed from those childhood years when her mother had seemed omnipotent, through the years of her own adulthood when she questioned her mother's judgment, to more recent times when her mother had become a maddening Medusa.

With the arrival of Sunday morning, she left her mother in the company of the nurse and returned to her townhouse, where she lethargically showered and dressed for church. She was depleted and drained, but she knew that she had a two-fold mission: to pray for her mother in the comforting solace of the sanctuary and to seek out Joe.

Her fingers went to her necklace, the black coral suspended between her breasts. The necklace might be a symbol of some future escape to paradise. But paradise could be had here, with the people she loved, if she took the time.

If that meant giving her mother physical therapy and taking care of her in her townhouse, she would do it. If that meant settling for mere friendship with Joe, she would. If he would only give her the opportunity.

Her prayer was easy. Facing Joe was more difficult. After services, she found him at the church's coffee bar. He looked tired. More than she, if that were possible. She quelled that cowardly urge to run and said, "May I talk to you? Privately?"

He nodded and followed her across the crowded salon, nodding to friends as they went. From his expression, she couldn't tell if she had any chance with him.

In a corner, the most secluded she could hope for at ten-thirty on a Sunday morning, she said, "I want to change, but it may be too late. We've lost our friendship. I want it back." She spread her hands in helpless despair and frustration. "What is wrong with me, Joe," she demanded, "that I have trouble with all the men I date?"

He set his half-empty cup on a table and took her hands in his. "If something's wrong with you, Sarah, I'm the wrong man to ask. I fell in love with you the first day we met."

Her mouth opened. "I thought I was . . . just your friend."

He leaned toward her and kissed her lightly, lovingly, in front of all the astonished church members. "You are. My friend and my lover, Sarah."

August 31—There really is such a thing as a soul mate. Wedding bells will ring today.

THE MAGIC TIME MACHINE
Rita Clay Estrada

For Theresa Behenna,
who gets as much emotion out of piano keys
as I try to do with words.
Thanks, friend.

Chapter One

Theresa stared at her best friend as if she'd just grown horns—or lost her mind. "Gayle, you're not making sense. You told me you wanted to treat me to lunch today. Now, you're informing me that you set me up to have lunch with a perfect stranger because you lost a bet?"

"He's not a 'perfect' stranger," Gayle tried to joke. "He's got problems, too."

"Don't we all," Theresa stated dryly in exasperation. "So why am I the lucky one to spend lunch with a gambling man?"

Gayle looked down at her water glass, took a deep breath, and began her explanation. "You probably don't remember him. His name is John Trainer, only now he's called J.D. He sat in back of us on the bus one year in high school."

The name sounded familiar, but nothing came

to mind. After all, she was thirty-six years old now. High school was a very long time ago, and some of the things that had happened long ago she preferred not to think about. Another lifetime. One dead marriage ago. "What happened then? Did he get a car?"

"No," Gayle admitted reluctantly. "He graduated."

A chill went down her spine at some earlier memory that wanted to break forth. "Graduated? He was riding the bus when he was a senior in high school?"

"Snob," her friend accused. "Not everyone's parents could afford a car."

"No, but most of us saved toward owning one." She knew. She knew, but she didn't want her knowledge confirmed. *Not John*, she prayed. *Not John!*

Gayle continued, ignoring her remark, "Don't you remember him? He was *huge* for his age. Some of the guys called him Big John, but not to his face. No one tried that."

Against her will, a picture of a manlike, gangly boy who looked as if he'd just come off the farm flashed through her mind. He used to get on the bus one stop after hers. Without saying a word, he'd sit behind her and Gayle for the twenty-minute drive to school. The first week he appeared she was uncomfortable. But as time passed, her feelings changed. His quiet demeanor gave her a sense of comfort. On the few occasions he was absent, she missed him. It took a long time before she found out his name—that fateful month before their high school Valentine's Day dance, to be exact.

"John," she mused, pretending to reach for the memory instead of admitting it was flooding her own mind. After twenty-two years, his features were a blur, all except for startling blue eyes that had the ability to see straight through her. "John Trainer."

"That's the guy," Gayle stated smugly, realizing her friend finally remembered. "And if he was good-looking then, you should see him now."

"Good-looking? I just thought he was big."

Gayle looked surprised. "You never noticed that strong jaw and pouting lower lip? Or that he had a neck resembling a redwood tree trunk, matching that wonderful, broad chest. Or—" her friend broke off.

Theresa took another bread stick from the basket and broke it in half. "If you remember him so well, why is it that I haven't heard about him before?"

"Because he moved away right after graduation. But he's back in Houston now and he's opened The Magic Time Machine restaurant, a sort of bar and playground for adults. Then he bought that wonderful tower home on the bayou."

"It's nice to know that one of our classmates made it big." Theresa sat back and stared sternly at her best friend across the luncheon table. "So how did I get included in this bet? And what was the bet about? And why did you bet me against a guy I can barely remember?"

Gayle's look was sharp, her voice droll. "Has someone else we know been divorced for three years with no new prospects in sight?"

"You know enough people to bet any number of women," Theresa stated firmly. "And there has to be a reason you'd take a chance on our friendship this way."

Gayle's face fell. "You're mad at me."

"Yes."

"*Really* mad."

"Yes."

Out of the corner of her eye, Theresa caught a blur of red. Without looking up, she felt the man standing beside her table. "Don't be mad, Theresa, or I'll think that all those hours patiently sitting behind you on the bus were a mistake instead of a reward." The voice was deep, flowing down her spine like icy water over a stony bed.

In slow motion, Theresa tilted her head up to see John Trainer holding a brilliant red rose. The man was twice as riveting as the rose.

The remnants of the young boy who rode to school in the seat behind her were still there but just barely. Hormones and time had hardened and rearranged his features into sexy granite. John Trainer was drop-dead gorgeous.

"John?" Her voice sounded as weak as he looked strong.

He grinned, creating two deep slashes that resembled a set of parentheses to his beautiful mouth. "I'm called J.D. now."

She felt her blush even before his gaze registered it. "By whom?" It was a smart retort, but no other words came to mind. Besides, sharp replies were her defense when she felt vulnerable. He almost stole her breath away.

"By new friends."

Gayle smiled beguilingly as she reached across the small restaurant table. J.D. took her hand and gave a light squeeze that sent a zing of jealousy up Theresa's back. She dismissed her reaction quickly.

Gayle sounded as flirty as her expression. "It's good to see you again, J.D. What have you been up to since last week?"

His smile was wonderful. "Waiting for *this* week."

Theresa smiled thinly. "What a shame. Life passes too quickly not to live it to the fullest."

"I do my best," John returned calmly, his gaze fluctuating between Gayle and Theresa. "Obviously, this is bad timing."

Gayle had the grace to look sheepish. "I haven't seen Theresa to tell her of our surprise until just a few moments ago," she said by way of an explanation. It seemed that he understood what she *hadn't* said.

"Don't worry, I think I see the problem," J.D. said quietly, his smile gone. "I'll leave you to your lunch. It's on me, of course."

Although Theresa hadn't wanted to be manipulated, she certainly hadn't wanted to reject him. "I'm sorry," she began.

But Gayle interrupted. "Sit down with us, J.D. There's certainly no need for you to eat alone."

Theresa felt his gaze rest on her but she couldn't look up. She didn't want to see his accusing look or feel the rapier sharpness of those blue eyes.

A long moment of silence passed. The restaurant noises finally penetrated their world; dishes clacking, distant laughter, the low hum of voices all blended together.

Theresa couldn't help it, but she looked up to be caught by the very eyes she hadn't wanted to see. He held her mesmerized. Once more she was sixteen and falling into the azure-blue gentleness of his gaze. Now they showed age, depth, wisdom, and a sadness only experience could produce.

"I think I'll pass, Gayle," he said slowly, his eyes still holding Theresa quiet. She could see his disappointment. But disappointment in what? Her? "But thanks anyway. It was a bad idea."

Before she realized it, J.D. Trainer was gone, weaving through the tables toward the front door.

"Well, you certainly know how to turn off a man," Gayle muttered angrily. "But couldn't you have chosen someone who plays the game better? At least someone else would have known the ground rules."

"The kind of man J.D. turned into makes his

own ground rules, Gayle." Theresa cleared her throat, trying to recapture her thoughts. "You had no right to set me up that way," she finally accused.

"I had every right," Gayle argued. "Ever since your divorce, you've been saying that you'd love to meet some of our old friends. Just three months ago we had lunch with Judy Russel, and it didn't seem to bother you that I invited her on the spur of the moment." Gayle leaned closer. "So tell me what bothers you about this meeting? Is it that John is a male? Or is it that John is someone from your past? Which?"

Theresa had the grace to be repentant. "I didn't mean to imply that it was a date setup."

But Gayle wasn't about to let her off the hook so easily. "But it *was* a date. And I *did* set it up. J.D. asked me and I didn't see any harm in having lunch with a guy you went to school with— especially a good-looking guy."

"You should have told me."

"Ahead of time?" Gayle asked, and Theresa nodded her head. "You wouldn't have met him. Besides, I didn't see any harm in a man buying you lunch and bringing you a rose"—Gayle nodded to the cellophane-wrapped flower on the table—"to celebrate the reunion of two old friends of the opposite sex."

Theresa knew she was over-reacting. After all, it wasn't Gayle's fault that Theresa's response to John was so strong. Gayle didn't know about the fiasco of a Valentine's dance lo those many years ago. Gayle had come down with mononucleosis, and had been home-bound without visitors for over three weeks.

Reaching across the table, she clasped her friend's hand. "I'm sorry. You're right, I'm acting silly. I let my emotions get out of hand. Forgive me?"

Gayle opened her mouth to reply. Instead, John's deep voice answered, "Gayle forgives you, but I don't. Not yet."

Theresa's eyes widened as she stared up at the man who had returned with a very determined look in his eye. "Excuse me, but I could have sworn you'd left."

"Oh, I did," he agreed. "Then I remembered that one of us was always leaving the other. This time I decided to take a new tack. If the old one didn't work then, it won't work now."

"What do you expect to happen?"

"I expect to get your attention."

"I don't like surprises."

"I'm not a surprise, I'm an old friend. Or don't you remember?"

Theresa felt her cheeks redden, but this time she refused to look away. "I remember," she said with as much dignity as she could muster.

Gayle leaned forward. "Theresa?"

She was asking to leave. Theresa gave in gracefully. "I'll see you next week," she promised her friend with a stiff smile.

Relief tinged Gayle's eyes as she stood and
planted a kiss on J.D.'s cheek. "I'll see you at the
club next week."

His grin was endearing, immediately reminding
Theresa of their youth.

"Right," he confirmed.

Then Gayle was gone, leaving only the scent
of her perfume to remind them she'd been there.
John—J.D.—took Gayle's seat, and Theresa stared
at him, waiting.

Her first impression was correct. He was too
handsome for his own good. And from the gleam
in his eye, she knew he was recalling the same
embarrassing memories she was.

She blushed again.

"I came back."

"So I see," she said, reaching for her glass of
water.

"It's my turn to claim you."

Her chuckle was brittle. "It's a little too late. I've
already been 'claimed.' "

"Charlie's gone." He shook his dark head slowly.
"Besides, it's never too late. I'll prove it to you."

Her breath caught in her throat at the promise
stated in those words. "Please," she began.

His hand covered her fingers holding the
chilled glass. "I turned down your invitation
once, Theresa, and you've turned down mine.
But now it's a new life and we're both smarter.
I'm back in town and in your life. I want to see
you again."

She slipped her hand from his and placed it in her lap. Without his touch, it felt oddly cold. "I don't want to see you."

He sighed. "You don't pull any punches, do you?"

Theresa hated to hurt him, but she wasn't into hurting herself anymore either. Those habits were gone. So were the years when she dreamed of being saved from herself by some white knight on a charging steed. "I'm sorry, John. It really is too late . . ."

"It's never too late," J.D. repeated softly. But she heard him clearly over the din of the restaurant. "I know what you went through after you married Charlie. But that's not the way it's supposed to be, Theresa. It's not even close."

Theresa's eyes widened from the unexpected hit her ex-husband's name caused in her midsection. "Charlie has nothing to do with this. We've been divorced for years."

"And for fifteen he treated you like dirt." J.D.'s voice verbalized his disgust.

"That's none of your business."

"Since I want to be with you, it is my business. I should have taken what you so generously offered that evening at the dance. But I didn't. Now, I'm asking that you offer it again. This time I won't let you walk away."

"You won't have that chance." Theresa stood, automatically reaching for the flower and holding it to her breast. "I'm sorry, I have to go."

"Don't."

It was only one word, spoken in a low voice she barely heard. But he could have screamed and gotten the same reaction. Panic invaded her every nerve.

She clutched her purse. "Don't," she repeated, knowing they were asking different things from each other.

Neither could deliver the results the other wanted.

She turned, and her heels clicked like castanets against the black-and-white tiles of the restaurant floor as she walked away. Keeping her stride, she pushed against the door, walked out, and went toward her car parked down a block.

She tried to lose herself in the rhythm of her walk. It didn't work. Her mind replayed the memory of the time she decided to attract John's romantic interest. It had been an unfair thing to do, but she'd done it. And her behavior had haunted her ever since.

Although Charlie was two years older than Theresa, he had been a part of her life since junior high school, when their mothers carpooled with each other. They began dating in the beginning of her sophomore year, when Charlie was a senior and had finally decided that she was worthy of his attention. She was madly in love, wondering how she had ever caught the attention of someone as cute and wonderful as he was. She blinded herself to his occasional fits of jealousy and temper tantrums. She had purposely not paid attention to his selfishness; she was always willing to go where *he* wanted to go, to do what *he* wanted to do. All wrongs and slights were forgotten once Charlie smiled at her.

Then came the night she had run into one of his friends in the grocery store parking lot and stopped to talk to him. Charlie had heard about it later and accused her of so many ugly things. No matter how much she explained that the meeting was innocent, Charlie had become angrier and angrier. Finally, he'd walked out and slammed the door, vowing at the top of his voice never to return.

Shaken, she ran to her room and cried her eyes out. Once, she tried to call Charlie, but he rudely hung up on her, although not before she heard a girl's giggling. That was the last straw! It was her turn to be angry, and her anger lasted a whole week. Then everything reversed, and Charlie was the one who wanted her back. During that time she refused all Charlie's phone calls and pleas at the front door.

Also during that week, she tried her just-fledged feminine wings of daring. And the object of her interest was John. Wonderful, even-tempered, quiet John. For five days she went out of her way to talk to him, batting her eyelashes, swaying her young hips, and in general, making a pest of herself.

John was kind, indulgent, and so very gentle

with her. She was never sure if he behaved that way because she was funny, or because he truly liked her. When he asked her to the Valentine's dance that Saturday, she was giddy with relief. Everyone knew she'd broken up with Charlie, but no one had asked her to go. Now her pride would remain intact. She could hold her head high and enter the decorated high-school gym on the arm of a guy. For a sixteen-year-old, it meant every-thing.

But, once John escorted her inside, she saw Charlie. Panic made her clutch John's arm tighter, smile brighter, and flirt outrageously. When John finally took her outside to cool off after a par-ticularly strenuous dance, she didn't realize just how strung out she was until he took her in his arms and kissed her. She'd been leading up to that moment all night, in the hopes that Charlie would see them together. What she hadn't been ready for was her own reaction.

She had been stunned. Unlike Charlie, John had kissed like a man, expecting her to react like a full-blown woman. She hadn't.

How could she forget that most humiliating moment? Instead of following through, she'd pulled back, stared up at him in wonder and confusion. He watched her carefully through narrowed lids. In a soft voice, he extended his dare. "Kiss me back."

Standing on tiptoe, she mashed her slightly part-ed mouth to his again.

When she pulled away, slightly breathless, he stared down at her from his great height, his dark blue eyes remote. "Someday you'll grow up, Theresa. Until then, I won't be used to make Charlie or anyone else jealous. I thought you knew better than that."

Confused at her own childish emotions, she'd lashed out. "I never asked you to kiss me. Besides, you're not as good as Charlie."

"Don't play games, Theresa. You asked with every movement," he'd answered, disgust lacing his voice. "And now you have something to compare that wilted jock to."

He'd turned and walked inside, leaving her in the dark. She'd been humiliated. His being right about her behavior had only made her feel worse. The darkness wasn't dark enough to swallow her up.

With a lot more bravado than she knew she had, she walked back into the dance—and into Charlie's arms. Back then, she was never sure if she went back to Charlie because she loved him or because she was afraid of the emotions John had churned up.

Theresa slipped into her car and drove out of the parking lot toward home. But her mind was still on the past.

She and Charlie stayed together after that. He began telling her how jealous he was of her and how much he loved her. Like the young girl she was, she took jealousy as a compliment instead of a childish reaction. Even though a little voice inside her head told her not to accept his explanations for his behavior, she did, anyway. She muffled the voice—almost forever.

John continued to sit behind her on the school bus every day for the rest of the school year, but she never looked him in the eye again. She couldn't. Instead, she pretended that he wasn't there—until he wasn't.

Rumor was that John had attended Baylor University and then gone on to some wonderful job that allowed him to travel all over the world. Occasionally, she heard news of him: John was living in Mexico; John was setting up offices in Spain and Italy; John was married; John was divorced four years later. Everything was digested, the school dance experience was relived, and then she purposely forgot him until the next piece of information filtered into her world.

Theresa pulled into her townhouse driveway and killed the engine, then entered the back door. The answering machine sat on the counter, its red, one-eyed stare blinked back at her, silently stating there were calls to be answered.

The voice she heard was Gayle's. "Theresa, please don't be mad at me. You know I'd never do anything to hurt you, but J.D.'s had a crush on you forever, and you could certainly use a little reaffirmation of your own femininity. Oh, not that you're not in good mental shape, you understand! It's just that you don't think you need a man in

Rita Clay Estrada

your life when that's probably *exactly* what you need. Men do more than fix faucets and change oil, you know." A second's silence followed, then, "Just consider going out with him, honey. I don't like the thought of you being alone for the rest of your life, no matter how much you say that's what you really want."

Theresa punched the button to rewind the tape. Gayle's worry about her was the same worry Theresa used to have. When she first left Charlie, she craved the peace that came with being the only adult in the household. Her seventeen-year-old daughter, Marie, lived in her own youthful world, doing her own thing. After graduation, Marie went off to college and Theresa was really alone. It took a long time to get used to that. But now she was, and she liked it that way.

It was only in the past year that her life had settled into a calm routine. Marie was in her sophomore year at University of Texas, and she was happy in Austin. At least Charlie and his new and very pregnant bride paid half the bills for Marie's schooling.

But according to Gayle, Theresa's life was in stall position. That was the reason for J.D.'s coming into her life. After twenty years, Theresa's youthful mistake had come back to haunt her. If she'd been embarrassed twenty years ago, she was even more so now.

J.D. Trainer needed to seek out another woman and turn those baby blue eyes on some other

106

dream-starved female. God only knew, he was top fantasy material.

With a heavy sigh, Theresa poured herself a glass of wine and sat in the living room, staring into the dark confines of the fireplace.

The emptiness of the house reminded her of the emptiness of her life. It wasn't due to the divorce. Heaven only knew, she'd been lonely all her life, *especially* when she was married. This odd, empty feeling was growing, though, and that was frightening. She wasn't sure how to cope with it.

She had tried all her life to be the kind of person others would like. She had tried to make Charlie a good wife so he would love her. With the exception of that one time when she had used John against Charlie, Theresa had tried never to hurt anyone. Yet, all her life, she'd never found her own happiness. Obviously, everything she'd done was wrong, or she would have received the reward she was promised as a kid. "Do good things and good things come to you." It was her mother's favorite saying.

Now she knew it wasn't true. Her child was grown, her husband had never loved her, her marriage was now dissolved, and her career had stalled.

No more! her thoughts screamed. But, for the first time, she was unable to stop the flow of tears for the death of her youth, lost dreams, and for what could have been. Her sobs echoed off the walls.

Rita Clay Estrada

Tears washed down her face like rain on glass. She couldn't stop crying. Her hands clenched into fists. Pain wracked her body as her muscles strained under the pressure. Theresa was finally taking the time to mourn the past so she could move on to the future. She knew that, but she hated every minute of it. . . .

Chapter Two

Magic Time Machine was scripted in bright pink, lavender, and blue neon over the entrance to the club. J.D. glanced up at it, just as he did every time he unlocked the entrance to his establishment. It gave him a sense of pride and an affirmation that he had succeeded in what he'd set out to do.

The inside was dark until he hit the switches that turned on the soft pastel lighting inside. He strode through the waiting area and into the first dining room. Although he still owned a few other restaurants and one or two neighborhood bars, this place was his dream come true. He'd toyed with the idea of having an outrageous club for some time, but it was only recently that he had been able to do it without selling off his other properties or going deeply into debt. And he owed it all to his father and an unexpected inheritance, bless his black heart.

He walked through the restaurant, passed the pool and shuffleboard area, disco, and video room on his way to the showroom. This was his favorite section. His two-story office was behind the ornate bar and a one-way window allowed him a view of the stage. All the other areas pivoted like a wagon wheel around this center room.

It was here that a casual dinner was served while patrons sat at tables on five different levels which allowed them to see the stage and the two-story screen attached to the wall behind it. A large podium sat in the middle of the stage, allowing customers to stand in front of their peers and sing songs, while a large background screen helped turn their creative efforts into a video they could take home as a souvenir. The system was called Karoke, and for a reasonable fee, anyone could be a star. The customers ate it up like popcorn; some enjoyed watching their friends while others needed to be the center of attention for a while.

He wondered what Theresa would think of it?

The thought intrigued him.

Once inside his office, he reached for the phone, quickly dialing the number he had never dialed before but knew by heart.

He felt his chest constrict at the sound of her voice. "Hi, Theresa. This is J.D."

Her own greeting was far more hesitant. "Hello. How are you?"

He wanted to get the politeness out of the way so he could ask her to be with him. In his arms. In his bed.

Instead, he answered politely, "I'm fine. How about you?"

Her answer was equally polite, and he enjoyed the sound of her low voice in his ear. His mind and body responded differently. Her tone was both soothing and arousing.

"We didn't have time to talk, to relax with each other. I want to do that. Have dinner with me." Even to his own ears it sounded like an order. Damn it!

"I'm sorry, I can't."

"Why not?"

"I work nights," she explained.

How could he have forgotten such an important part of her—her piano? In fact, he'd even gone to the hotel bar where she worked and found a table in a darkened corner and listened to her play. He silently cursed himself before speaking. "But not days, right?"

A moment's hesitation. "Right."

"Good. Then have lunch with me tomorrow."

"John, I . . ."

He remembered Gayle's warning about rushing her, and tried to soft pedal his request. "J.D., and don't say no. There's no reason for two old friends not to have lunch and enjoy a pleasant hour."

"I—"

111

"And I pledge not to mention my unfulfilled youthful fantasies if you promise to tell me all of yours."

She couldn't help the smile in her tone of voice. His sense of humor was so unexpected—and so nice. "I don't think that's a good idea."

"Why not? It sounds like an even exchange to me. Mine are obvious or I wouldn't be pursuing you. Yours, however, are so deeply buried by now that you need to release them so they can find their way to fruition."

He finally got a full-blown chuckle out of her. "For someone who's so dead pan and conservative-looking, you have a certain bent to your sense of humor," she retorted.

"Yes, and yes." He took a deep breath, wondering what she would think if she knew how unconservative his thoughts about her were right now. "I'll pick you up at noon. Dress casually and relax. I never bite on the first date. Especially if the lady is a friend."

"Okay," she relented. "But let me meet you instead of your going to the bother of picking me up."

She really was scared. He wondered what had made her so fragile that she needed to be in control of her comings and goings. He promised himself that he would find out before the week was over.

"It's fine by me," he said casually. "We'll eat here, at the Magic Time Machine. That way I can work until you get here. To make up for it, I'll give you the grand tour."

"That sounds great. I haven't had a chance to see it yet," she answered, and he heard the relief in her voice. "I'll be there at twelve."

When J.D. hung up the phone, his face split into a grin. His grin widened. Then he downright laughed out loud. Theresa was coming to his club. If he played his hand right, she'd come again— and again. And slowly, he'd win her over until she thought *his* way of thinking was *her* way of thinking. . . .

Theresa stared into the mirror and wondered what in heaven's name she was doing.

"It's too late now," she told the image staring solemnly back at her. "Fun" wasn't a word the woman in the mirror seemed familiar with. She looked presentable if that counted for anything. Her short red hair was slightly curled behind her ears, framing her face well. A hot pink jumpsuit showed off her figure. A pair of multi-colored flats coordinated the outfit.

"Get going," she muttered aloud, resolutely turning her back on the image and grabbing her purse. "This is only lunch, not a pagan ceremony with sacrificial victims."

Although Houston was big, it wasn't big enough to stall her progress. She was at J.D.'s place in fifteen minutes. Only six or seven cars were in the side parking lot. It dawned on Theresa that the restaurant itself was probably not open for lunch.

Her nerves tightened in warning.

She pulled on the handle of the door to the club and it opened easily. She wanted it to open, but, conversely, she also hoped it would be locked.

Gayle had told her about the concept behind J.D.'s club, but this was the first time she'd been inside. Gayle had been right. It was an adult child's wonderland.

As she took in the carnival atmosphere of the front hall, muffled footsteps came toward her.

"Welcome to the Magic Time Machine." J.D.'s voice was deep and low and held just a hint of laughter.

Suddenly Theresa felt shy. "Thank you." She glanced around the empty room again. "You aren't usually open for lunch, are you?"

"For you I am."

There it was again. That sexy voice that spoke as if she were the only person in the world. When she heard it, she felt warm and special and then she was swamped with pure, unadulterated panic.

Theresa swallowed hard and pasted a light smile on her mouth. She wanted this lunch finished so she could go home and feel safe again. "I'm starved!"

J.D.'s hand curved around her upper arm and he led her into the formal dining area to a table in the corner with a view of the entire room. Like all the other tables, it was set with a forest-green and brick-red tablecloth and napkins, matching the rest of the decor.

Theresa sat down in the seat J.D. pulled out, then he sat next to her. Within seconds, a young waiter brought out a bottle of white wine and, with a broad grin, poured them each a glass.

J.D. lifted his glass. "To many more luncheons to while away the noonday hours."

"To today," she compromised before taking a sip. The wine was perfect.

"I took the liberty of ordering our meal ahead of time." His gaze lightly touched her face. "I hope you don't mind, but I wanted as much time with you as possible."

"As long as it's not liver or kidneys, I'm fine," she admitted.

He grinned endearingly. "It's fresh flounder in a light crab sauce."

"Sounds great." Curiosity overcame her natural reticence. She set down her glass and stared at him, her brow furrowing in confusion. "J.D., why me?"

He didn't pretend to misunderstand. "I thought you would have realized by now that I go after what I want."

The waiter returned, placing a crisp, Caesar salad in front of each of them. After fresh ground pepper was dispensed and the waiter left, the silence between them stretched interminably.

Theresa couldn't look at J.D. anymore. Instead, she took her fork and played with a leaf of her salad, pretending she had nothing more important on her mind. Pretending that she hadn't heard his declaration and it hadn't affected her.

"Theresa." He spoke her name softly.

She was captivated when she looked up, snared by his gorgeous, blue-eyed gaze.

"Theresa." He said it again, this time in a lower tone.

Her heart softened, melting a few of the walls she'd thrown up over the years.

"Theresa."

This time it was a whisky-rough whisper that caressed her skin.

His gaze delved into her, and she felt as if her emotions were vulnerable and exposed. Surprisingly, she wasn't threatened. They were in another time, another life. They were young and slightly defiant and living on the edge of emotion again.

Once more she was a teenager, trying to snare the man who intrigued her even while she was dating the boy who was safe. New and untried ways of making him notice her were flowing through her mind. Needs and wants were keen still, not tempered with the knowledge of years and heartache.

Theresa realized that the boy she had chosen to marry couldn't really hurt her deeply because he was only a child himself. But John was different. She had the feeling he had always been an adult. John had always been different. . . .

"Why me?" she asked again, needing an answer

that would give her a clue to her own personality.

He shrugged, a small smile tugging at his sensuous mouth. "It's always been you," he said. "The gods must have rolled the dice and you and I bounced up."

Her heartbeat raced in the pulse in her throat. "They have a weird sense of humor."

"It seems just about right to me."

"We don't fit."

Her throaty protest was brushed aside. "We don't have to. Fitting isn't what we're about, Theresa. We're two adult and very different people who have led entirely different lives. Now is the time to bring our own special talents together and see what we can create."

Her breath was so shallow she wasn't sure she was breathing at all. "Are you expecting us to make great music together?"

This time he chuckled outright. "Hardly. Crashing cymbals. Lots of percussion. Maybe even a sour note now and then. If we didn't hit those, we wouldn't be playing."

"I don't understand."

"As long as we play in the game of life, we'll make wrong notes. We'll also make right ones. It's up to us to create what we want. The more we work on this relationship, the more mistakes we'll make. And the closer we'll become." He leaned forward and her breath caught in her throat. "The more mistakes we make together, Theresa, the more we know we're trying to succeed. No one blunders when they're doing nothing."

"You're talking as if we're creating a relationship," she protested. "I'm not willing to get involved, J.D."

"What are you willing to do?"

She became flustered, dropping her fork to the table with a muffled clatter. "Nothing. You asked me for lunch. I couldn't refuse without being made the villain in this piece. So I accepted."

"You have to get involved, Theresa, even if we're only talking about friendship."

"J.D.," she faltered.

Saved by the food, he thought as the waiter brought their plates and set them down by the salads. It was time to back away. She needed time to digest this conversation before he asked more of her.

"I think you'll like this," he commented easily. "It's one of my favorites."

From that moment on, J.D. kept all conversation on a casual level. Slowly, ever so slowly, he watched her relax. Her smiles came more frequently, her body eased against the chair back, and her beautiful eyes danced with occasional laughter.

Theresa began to contribute to the conversation. " . . . but I realized I didn't like gambling when the roulette wheel took my last silver dollar. It's not a kind sport."

"Did Charlie like gambling?"

Her expression closed. "I guess so."

"He was a part of your life, Theresa. We should be able to bring up his name without your getting tense. Friends talk about all the parts of their lives, not just a limited few." J.D. leaned back, his gaze never leaving her face. "Look. I've always wanted to be your friend. That hasn't changed. I still do. Is that impossible?"

She was wary, her gaze guarded. "No, of course not. But . . ."

"And we all need friends, right?"

"Right."

"And friends discuss all kinds of things and tell each other what they're feeling. Right?"

"Right."

"Good. Then we can be friends?"

"Of course we can," she said, relaxed and smiling. "If you still want to, so do I."

He leaned back. "Good. Now, did Charlie like gambling?"

"He loved it, but we never had enough money left over to fulfill his fantasy of going to Las Vegas every two or three months to parley his money into millions."

"Tell me about your marriage."

She looked up, startled.

"It's a topic friends talk about, Theresa," he reassured her. "Let's get it out of the way now."

She took a dainty bite of her fish. He'd bet his last club acquisition that she didn't taste it.

"There's nothing much to say. I thought I was

in love with Charlie. I wasn't. It took a child and many years of living with him to teach me that."

"Did Charlie think he was in love, too?"

She shrugged. "He must have. He proposed."

"I proposed, too, but I wasn't in love. I was just ready to be married."

Her brown eyes stared at him, touching his heart with their sadness. "Didn't you think you could hurt your wife by living a lie?"

"I wasn't living a lie. I was a married man who kept his vows."

"Not loving her was making a mockery out of them."

He frowned, wondering how concerned she was about his marriage—and how frustrated she felt about her own. "Carly knew when we married that I was committed to making the marriage work. She also knew that I wasn't in love with her but I respected her and enjoyed her company. We both hoped it would work out. Three years later we gave up and went our separate ways."

"Do you still see her?" Theresa asked.

J.D. nodded. "She was at the opening of the Magic Time Machine and has had dinner here once in a while. We're still good friends."

"Do you miss married life?"

"Yes." J.D. sat forward. "Do you?"

Her expression was melancholy. "Yes."

He placed his hand over hers, giving a light squeeze. "Charlie always had short vision, never seeing the gold right under his nose."

Her smile didn't make it to her beautiful brown eyes. "Charlie was my husband."

"That doesn't relegate him to sainthood. In fact, he richly deserves a kick in the—"

"Careful," she said, a small smile peeping through. "He was my choice. If you blacken him too much, it means that I didn't have the good judgment to choose well."

J.D. grinned back. "Yes, but what does a sixteen-year-old know about choices? You hadn't even developed a sense of taste yet."

Her eyes widened. "Were you always this wise?"

He nodded solemnly. "Yes. I was even wise enough not to tell you what I thought about him when I wanted to the most."

"When was that?"

"When I kissed you."

Red tinged her cheeks, but she raised her chin as she answered. "When I forced you into kissing me," she said tightly. "That was a long time ago, J.D. So long ago I hardly remember it."

He grinned. "Liar."

Her smile peeped out. "Okay, so I lied. I was embarrassed to tears then. I'm still embarrassed."

"I wasn't embarrassed," he confessed. "I was stunned. Your touch knocked me over like Paul Bunyan's felled tree. I could hardly put a coherent thought together, let alone tell you how I felt."

Theresa laughed. "Sure. And would you like to pull my other leg?"

"I mean it, Tess," he said, using her old nickname and watching for her reaction. There was none. "You were so innocent and childlike and womanly, all wrapped up in one dynamite package. You scared the hell out of me because I didn't think you knew what you were doing and how well you were succeeding."

Her eyes widened until he couldn't look away. "Are you teasing me?"

"No." He took a deep breath. He needed to stay as close to the truth as he could without scaring her again. He could tell her the rest, later. "I think I might have had a crush on you and didn't know it back then. I was jealous of Charlie way before the Valentine's dance. When you kissed me, I wasn't sure I could stop myself from grabbing you and kissing you back. If I had, I might have scared the hell out of you, and I wouldn't have hurt you for the world."

Theresa leaned back and stared at him in amazement. "Do you mean to tell me that I've felt guilty for playing the femme fatale all these years for nothing?"

His grin widened as he nodded his assent. "I guess so. I didn't know you felt guilty or I would have returned sooner and told you the truth."

Her laughter was warm and wonderful to hear. "You've done enough already," she assured him, her cinnamon-brown eyes alight with delight. "You've made my day."

"Happy to oblige, ma'am. Are you ready for

some sinfully delicious chocolate dessert and fresh coffee?"

"After that little declaration, I'm ready for anything," she assured him.

J.D. grinned. "Perhaps. But we'll still take it one step at a time, just in case," he said, motioning to the waiter standing by the kitchen door.

No sense frightening Theresa yet. She was just beginning to relax. He wanted to make sure she relaxed enough so that he could make her fall in love with him. He was going for greater stakes. He wanted her to spend the rest of her life with him.

J.D. Trainer wanted it all. . . .

Chapter Three

People milling around the lobby of the exclusive Diamond Hotel looked as if they were ready to slow down and relax after a hectic day. The hotel had five different conventions going on at the same time. It wasn't a particularly unusual set of circumstances, but it did mean that there was a lot of hustle and bustle in the hotel.

Theresa waved at Sigried, the restaurant manager, as she headed toward the cozy, pub-like atmosphere of the hotel bar. A beautiful grand piano sat in the center of the room, barstools circling all but the musician's seat. Mirrors reflected dim light through the room. Low club chairs with even smaller tables filled all but the postage-stamp dance floor.

According to her new contract, this pub would be her professional home for another six months. After that, she didn't know if she would sign a contract with the same pub again or audition for a job with another. Her agent would help her decide the next move when the time was near. But for now, this was her home away from home.

One of the waitresses came over and set a glass of champagne on the side of the piano. Theresa flashed her a thank you smile.

Taking out a notebook filled with music, Theresa placed it on the topside of the piano in case one of the patrons wanted to leaf through it and request a particular song.

Once everything was ready, Theresa sat down at the keyboard and let her fingers move across the keys in a lilting warm-up exercise as she smiled at each and every patron as if he or she were sitting in her living room. Their response was immediate—a big smile in return.

Two of her regular customers stood at the bar. One of them spoke up, "Glad you got here, Theresa. It was lonely without you."

She winked, comfortable in her surroundings. Bantering with customers was a part of her job. "You're just partial to good playing, Frank," she teased, edging into a song he often requested.

As the evening passed, people wandered in and out. Some were patrons of the bar and lived in town, others were guests of the hotel. Theresa talked to them all, chatting back and forth. She enjoyed the byplay. She also enjoyed playing the piano.

Five years ago she was a housewife, occasionally playing for private parties. Her divorce had forced her to find a regular income. Until then, she had only dreamed of playing professionally for a living. Playing four nights a week allowed her to support herself and help her daughter. But she occasionally wished she'd started out at a younger age. Several of her peers had traveled the world, played cruise ships and hotels that others only dreamed of visiting.

One of the men seemed to have read her mind. "You've got it made, lady," he said with a slight slur. "You don't have to fight traffic every morning and evening. You don't have to worry about the office staff bumping you off or talking behind your back. You don't even have to think about all the crap that goes on in the real world."

Theresa forced herself to flash him a smile. Where in the world did he think she lived—in never-never land? Everyone had bills, dirty sheets, and all the other things that were a part of living. "That's right," she murmured. "I'm the lucky one."

The woman on his right managed to divert him and Theresa slipped into the next song, an old number she remembered her mother loving to hear. Now her mother was visiting Australia. . . .

She glanced up and her gaze was caught by J.D. standing in the entrance. With sure steps, he walked toward her and took the empty stool directly at the end of the piano. He winked and flashed her an intimate smile. "Hi, friend," he said.

"Hi." Her heart jump-started into a new rhythm. She suddenly felt clumsy. Calling her a friend helped ease the awkwardness but remnants still remained. He was J.D. Big and impressive and no longer the gangly, young boy. J.D. Trainer was all man.

Quietly, he ordered a drink from the appreciative waitress, then focused his attention completely on her.

Once more—just like when she was a teenager on the bus—the awkwardness left, replaced by an unbelievable confidence in her ability to do her best. She swung from pop to classical and back to pop again. She was at her peak and she knew it.

But, occasionally there was a drunk to keep in line. Tonight was one of those nights.

"Okay, Theresa, it's time to play *Melancholy Baby*, only sing it with the dirty lyrics," he slurred, almost spilling his drink with the effort of talking. "A good-looking woman like you should know all the dirty lyrics."

She saw the tightness around J.D.'s mouth. This meant war, if she was reading him right. Theresa caught his eye and gave a brief shake of her head. J.D. saw the motion, but the thunderous expression darkening his gaze didn't waver.

She smiled brightly at the inebriated man and ran her fingers over the keys before beginning the next dreamy ballad. "And what part of the country does your rock reside?"

A few of the patrons laughed. But not J.D. "Huh?"

"She's saying you crawled out from under a rock, buddy," one of the customers volunteered. "And I agree. Go sober up somewhere."

The drunk stared hard at the man who spoke, then shrugged his shoulders and stood. Balancing very carefully, he walked out of the pub.

Theresa gave a sigh of relief, not because she couldn't handle the lush, but because she couldn't handle J.D. if he decided to do something foolish. Just minutes ago, the heat of his anger had slammed into her. It was wrong to think of him as a gentle giant. Once fired up, he would be hard to control. It was a dangerous thought.

The rest of the evening went smoothly. Theresa played the audience, received several large bills in her cut-glass tip bowl, and watched J.D. like a hawk for any change in mood. It was amazing that she read him so well. It was also scary. She'd never been able to do that with anyone before. Had her subconscious made a connection with him that the rest of her didn't know about or have control over?

After the last tune, she said her good-byes, picked up her book, tips, and purse, and left. J.D. took it for granted that he would escort her to the hotel garage and walked by her side. She noticed that none of the patrons who were usually

Rita Clay Estrada

so possessive of her said anything to J.D.

Once Theresa reached her car, she turned and, holding the music binder in front of her like a shield, looked up at him. "Thank you for walking me out."

"I'm following you home."

She shook her head. "That isn't necessary."

"It is for me."

His whisky-husky voice washed over her, warming every inch of her body. "I—"

"I'll see you there."

"You're not coming in," she warned.

"I'm just insuring your safe ride home."

Theresa shrugged as if it didn't matter. "If you want to." In seconds she had unlocked her car door and slipped in. How J.D. found her place was up to him. She wasn't waiting around to lead him there by the hand.

Without a backward glance, she pulled out of the parking lot and into the stream of traffic. Fifteen minutes later she turned into her townhouse driveway and killed the engine, a smile on her face. J.D. hadn't been able to keep up with her. She'd lost him at the first turn. That was fine with her, she told herself.

Just as she got to her front door, headlights came down the street, then his brand-new Cadillac pulled in behind her car. J.D. stepped out of the car, leaving the engine running.

Theresa's happiness level rose ten points and she was irritated at her own reaction. It was tough

130

to crow about losing him when she really wanted him beside her. With her. She squelched the rest of her thoughts that cried for release.

He walked up to her and reached for her arms, his warm hands caressing her skin. The chill of the January night air swirled around them. Houston's weather had been warmer in the afternoon and neither was wearing an overcoat.

He spoke, but his mind wasn't on his words. "You drive like a maniac."

"I drive fast but safe," Theresa corrected firmly.

"You tried to lose me." It wasn't an accusation. He seemed more interested in the texture of her skin and the color of her eyes than in his statement.

"I knew where I was going and drove accordingly."

His grin was electric, even under her dim lamp light. She couldn't help her own answering smile.

"You're really something," he said, and she knew it wasn't her driving that he was referring to.

"So are you."

He lost some of his smile. "Do customers razz you often?"

"Often enough for me to know how to handle them. Alone."

"I don't like it."

He sounded so proprietorial. "That's my business, J.D. Not yours. I don't need your protection."

131

"Somebody needs to protect you from idiots like that."

"Yes. Me. Occasionally a bartender or my employer. But this isn't the caveman days where I need you to lean on. I take care of myself." She took a deep breath. "If you can't handle that, friend, then I suggest we don't see each other again."

She had his full attention. "You *are* tough."

"Right," she drawled sarcastically, but her pulse accelerated. She needed to be her own woman, but a part of her wanted, craved, to see him again. What if he couldn't handle her independence? Would she be strong enough not to see him?

He smiled slowly, his eyes filled with the dawning of understanding. "You're right, Theresa. It's not my business to protect you. It *is* my option to give you my protection should you need it."

"I'll remember that." It was a compromise that made her glad.

With his thumb, J.D. tilted her face up to his. "You're beautiful, determined, talented, and smart. You're really very unique."

Her mouth parted as she fastened her gaze on him. "Thank you."

His arms swung around to her back, lightly pulling her toward him. "Dear sweet heaven."

Her heart knew what she wanted. She knew what *he* wanted. Before she could talk herself out of it, she stood on tiptoe and gently placed her lips on his. It was a delicate touch, but once their lips met, she didn't want to stop the contact. His warm mouth molded to hers, his touch firm but gentle. She forced herself to pull away.

"My God," he muttered, sounding as awed by his reaction as she was with her own. They stared at each other for one long moment.

His hands tightened on her back, pulling her into the strength of his embrace again. This time, when his mouth covered hers, he was in full command. His lips were warm and firm, molding hers to the desired shape.

His arms held her tightly, pulling her into his body. Theresa leaned against him, fitting him to perfection, curve against bend, softness against hardness. A thousand sensations zinged through her senses—too many to pay attention to. Her hands slid up his chest, past his broad shoulders, and rested on the sides of his head, her fingers tangling in his crisp hair.

His mouth moved over hers as if he wanted to devour all of her—and she wanted him to. Excitement washed through her as she imagined them making love.

One large hand cupped her breast, weighing it, feeling her budding nipple harden at his touch. She couldn't stop the moan in her throat.

He pulled her closer and his own swollen manliness rested exactly where it should, between her thighs. So tempting. Theresa was experienced enough to know he wanted not just anyone. He wanted *her*. She wanted him. In her arms, in her bed. Now.

Warning bells pealed in her head, telling her of the danger she was in. She ignored them. His thumb passed over her nipple and she moaned again.

Heat flowed to the pit of her stomach like burning coal. Her hips undulated. This time, it was *his* moan that echoed in her mouth and she felt a measure of satisfaction. At least she wasn't alone with this building need.

Warning bells turned to sirens.

Theresa pulled away reluctantly. The cold air touched her lips where his warm, damp mouth had been, giving her a chill. Her eyelids drooped with sensual languor. She tilted her head and stared up at him.

"Dear sweet heaven," she murmured, repeating his own earlier words. One French-tipped fingernail traced his jaw line to the bottom of his full lip.

"I don't want you to misunderstand me, Theresa. I want to make love to you."

"J.D., I . . ." Her mind wasn't working.

His hands tightened slightly. "Tell me what you want, Theresa."

"I . . ." She couldn't think.

"Do we stay at your place or go to mine?"

The last time she'd been kissed like that she was a teenager. Since then, Charlie had always made the decision of when they were going to make love. He had taken the reins and guided her where he wanted to go. She had never chosen to take the lead. Her ex-husband had never asked her opinion or her permission.

J.D. sighed heavily. "What's going on in that beautiful head of yours, Theresa?"

"I don't know what to say," she finally admitted. "I didn't think—"

"Don't tell me. You expect me to make those decisions alone."

Her eyes were wide as she stared up at him, her hands still resting on his shoulders. "I don't know what I expect, J.D. You took me by surprise. I never imagined I'd have such an explosive reaction."

He brushed a strand of her hair away from her face so gently it felt as if a warm breeze had touched her. "I always knew we were a dangerous combination. I didn't realize that you weren't emotionally ready for it."

"What do you mean?"

"I mean that you're still an adolescent when it comes to the next step in this relationship. You want me to take the decision-making out of your hands." He looked so sad. His blue eyes were gray. "I can't do that."

"That's unfair," she whispered, even while knowing he was right on target. She couldn't dispute his words.

"To whom?" he asked quietly. "I want you more than words can say. But it has to be mutual,

Theresa. It has to be an adult decision that both of us agree to and want. Until then, nothing will happen between us."

Theresa didn't know whether she was happy or sad. She wanted him so much. There was a wonderful, sensuous pressure building inside her that only he could assuage. But that meant making a decision before she was ready, before she knew answers to a thousand questions. She wanted him to care for her as much as she was trying *not* to care for him. . . .

J.D. sighed again and Theresa felt his chest muscles tighten. "Okay, Theresa. I'll tell you what. You call me whenever you want to talk. Any time of the day or night. I'll talk to you all you want, whenever you want." He placed a soft, butterfly kiss on her forehead. "But until you decide that you want me as a woman wants a man, we won't see each other. When you're ready, come to the Magic Time Machine."

She wanted him so badly. But fear of showing those feelings warred with the emotions boiling beneath the surface. "Why are you making me do this?"

"Because I love you, Theresa." His voice was as low and as sad as hers. "I've always loved you. But I want to be with you like two adults, not like two teenagers. I'm too old for that and so are you. Games don't work anymore. Not when we're talking about being together for ever."

Her mind froze. Still stuck on the first words

he said, she barely registered the last ones. "You love me?"

He nodded.

Heat seared through her body. "Since when?"

"Ever since I can remember."

"Why didn't you say something?"

His smile was sad. "When? When you were going with Charlie and thought I was a big, dumb farmer-boy? After you married him and I knew the marriage was being destroyed by the way he treated you? Or when you were pregnant with his child and I went nuts thinking of you in his arms?"

Her fingers tightened on the fabric of his shirt. "I didn't know."

"I couldn't tell you then. But that doesn't solve our problem now, does it?"

Still, Theresa couldn't think. Her body still felt the effects of his kiss, but her mind refused to allow her to lead the way to a more intimate relationship.

J.D.'s hands tightened. "I'll talk to you tomorrow," he said slowly, then kissed her forehead. "Good night, Theresa."

Before she could protest, he was back in his car. She stood at her front door, chilled to the bone. It had more to do with J.D.'s absence than the chill January wind.

J.D. stuck his head out the window. "Go inside while I'm here," he ordered.

Like a robot, she did as she was told. He didn't drive away until she was inside with the door closed. She hadn't realized just how cold she was until she reached the safety of her entryway. Rubbing her arms, she brought some semblance of warmth to her limbs. Within minutes, she had turned on every light downstairs.

If only she could bring to light answers to the endless questions and problems circling her mind. Right now, she felt frustrated and hungry. And it was all because of J.D.

J.D. drove down the darkened street, a sinking feeling growing deep in the pit of his stomach. He had forced Theresa to make a decision about their relationship too quickly. She'd only just gotten used to seeing him, and now he was telling her he loved her.

He grimaced in the dark confines of the car. Love was a tame word compared to what he felt. It was as if he'd known her forever. His love was so deep and true that, if he believed in reincarnation, he'd swear that they'd been together in another lifetime.

And now he had just ruined his chances of making her fall in love with him by rushing her. Damn it! His fist hit the steering wheel. He should have shown a little patience. Hell, who was he kidding? He should have had a *lot* of patience! He'd been planning this move ever since he'd first found out she was finally divorced from that jerk, Charlie. Now, after all that planning, he might have blown it.

Every instinct in him wanted to turn around and head back to her place. He needed to tell her not to be so frightened. That it was all right to approach a man—as long as *he* was the man. He wanted to hold her once more, reassure her that it would be all right.

Just about now, her imagination would be going haywire, frightening her even more.

He pulled into his driveway, flicking the small switch that opened the black, wrought-iron gate. Impatient, he drove his car in, barely missing the metal. He parked in the driveway, flicked the switch to close the gate, and went in the back door to the breakfast area of the large three-storied house.

Set in the woods of Memorial area, it was secluded, peaceful, and everything he'd always dreamed of owning and could now afford. He'd fallen in love with it the moment he saw it.

Tonight, however, it wasn't important. He picked up the portable phone from its cradle and dialed Theresa's number. When she answered, he gave a sigh of relief.

"Are you all right?"

"I'm fine." Her voice sounded distant, just as he'd known it would.

"Whether we remain friends or become more intimate, Theresa, please don't lie."

Silence hung on the line between them. "You scare me," she finally admitted. "Right now, even my own reactions frighten me."

He leaned against the kitchen counter. "I know. It's all so new for you."

"Are you scared, too?"

"Only of losing contact with you."

"Why are you telling me this? If I wanted to hurt you, it would be so easy."

"Being honest is a double-edged sword, Theresa. If I'm not honest, you'll never know me—the real me few people ever see. Then, no matter who I love, I'd be alone. Knowing me well also means that you can hurt me as no one else can. But it's a chance I have to take."

"Why are you willing to take that chance?" Her voice was hesitant, disbelieving.

He sighed, hearing her fear and feeling his own heart pump heavily in confession. "I've loved you too long to lie about anything now."

"What do you want from me?" She was wary, but he could tell her curiosity was piqued.

"You. With me. Telling me that's where you want to be, too."

Holding his breath, he waited tensely. Her long silence seemed to stretch on forever. Then there was a click, another click, and the dial tone.

She had hung up on him.

His first response was to dial her back, but he knew better than that. Instead, J.D. very quietly hung up the phone, grabbed a glass from the cabinet, and headed for the library. Once there, he poured himself a stiff drink and sat down in the leather wingback chair facing the floor-to-ceiling window overlooking the side garden.

Quietly, a tear found its path down his cheek to his chin.

He'd taken the gamble.

He'd lost.

Chapter Four

Theresa trembled as she pulled her hand away from the phone in the cradle. She wished she was shaking this way because of the cold. If that were the case, she could wrap up in a blanket and it would go away in a few minutes. Or because of fear. Then she could talk herself out of it or call the police or tell her best friend.

But this reaction was from hunger. Emotional hunger such as she'd never known before. She didn't know how to cope with it or what to do to erase it.

J.D. brought it out in her, uncovering thoughts, feelings, and responses she never knew she was capable of. He touched her, and she shook in reaction. He kissed her, and she wanted to wrap her limbs around him and never let him go. He spoke of loving, and she pirated every word so she could hoard it like a precious jewel, treasuring its depth and brilliance when she was alone again.

But she was afraid to let him know how she felt. In some odd, twisted way, it was easier to be unhappy than it was to know that the one you love might reject you. And that was her biggest fear. What if they became involved and Theresa irrevocably lost her heart to J.D.? And what if J.D. didn't love her as much as she loved him, and he decided to end their relationship?

It was three o'clock in the morning before she closed her eyes. And then her dreams were erotic and exasperating.

When she woke up at noon, all she could think of to describe her feelings was that she was lonely. But not lonely for just anyone. Only J.D. would do. Damn the man!

By three o'clock she was a bundle of nerves, keeping herself from picking up the phone and telling him she'd meet him wherever he wanted.

In the past, hard physical labor had been a panacea. She began scrubbing the bathroom floor. Working hard for over an hour tired Theresa out but didn't stop the erotic thoughts of J.D. churning in her head.

It all came down to one question. Did she want to see him again?

The answer resounded in her head like a loud scream. Yes!

Was she willing to take the chance of being with

him, knowing that they might well end up in each other's arms—in bed? Making love?

Again, the answer was, yes but fear and excitement rushed through her, too.

However, it took a week to find the nerve to call J.D. and let him know of her decision. She finally gathered her mettle one morning after a full pot of strong coffee with enough caffeine to make her fly under her own steam.

The phone in his office rang two, three, four times before J.D.'s clipped tone came over the receiver. He didn't identify the restaurant or himself.

Instead, he repeated the number she had dialed. "J.D.?"

"Theresa." He recognized her voice immediately. "I was afraid you'd never call."

"Don't be so honest," she chided, suddenly feeling as if a bubble of light was caught inside her. Happiness was instantaneous.

"Why not? I'm asking for a relationship that allows that from both of us. I told you. I want extraordinary—not ordinary."

"Can we take this one step at a time?"

"Of course. Let's start with lunch today."

So much for slow, she thought wryly. "Where?"

"Here." He hesitated. "Do you bowl?"

"Not in a long time," she admitted.

"Dress casual. Do you want me to send a driver for you?"

"No, I . . ." Panic was swamping her again.

145

"Come soon. I'll be waiting." Then the line went dead.

Theresa swallowed down her fear as she glanced at her watch. She had exactly an hour to turn into a great-looking Cinderella-ready-for-the-bowl instead of princess-of-the-commode.

However, she made it with five minutes to spare. Her heart raced as fast as her car's engine as she drove to the Magic Time Machine. Taking a deep breath, she tried to tell herself that she could call their relationship off if she lost her nerve at the final moment. J.D. was not a mean or spiteful man. He wouldn't pursue her if she backed away once more.

Walking through the front door, she felt transported to another time and place, one where magical things happened and fun was all around.

J.D. stood just inside the door, his blue eyes narrow and bright as he watched her walk in. His gaze warmed her insides and she smiled. When she had come within inches of him, she stopped.

He touched her cheek. "Hi, beautiful." His voice was rich and deep and warm like heated honey flowing over her.

"Hi, handsome."

His blue eyes flared, then narrowed. He leaned forward and down, lightly brushing her mouth with his.

Excitement sped along her spine. She wanted him to continue, to make the kiss real. Instead, J.D. pulled back and smiled. His hands framed

her face, his thumbs gently soothing her cheeks.
"You're trembling."

"Am I?" She was surprised. She hadn't noticed.

"Are you really that frightened of me?"

She covered his hands with her own, loving the
feel of them on her skin. "No."

"Excited?"

Her lashes fell, then opened again to reveal what
she felt. "Yes." It was a simple statement, but it
came from her heart.

His lips brushed hers again. "Don't worry. So
am I."

Without another word, he turned. Holding her
hand, J.D. led her through the formal dining
room, through the video game room, around a
dais speakeasy bar, and into a bowling alley. In
front of one of the alleys was a clothed table set
with picnic cutlery and large mugs.

"A picnic?"

He grinned. "Sort of. I refuse to eat on plastic,
so we had to improvise. But I did allow paper
napkins."

"How big of you," she said dryly, thinking of
her own closet full of the offending critters. "Are
they recyclable?"

"Of course!" He turned to the counter, where
a young man in a tuxedo shirt with red tie and
cummerbund stood. "What's your shoe size?" he
asked.

Theresa told him, and the young man reached
for two pairs of bowling shoes, then came and

placed them on the bench in front of the alley
J.D. had chosen ahead of time.

From the moment she put on her bowling shoes,
she felt as if she was someone else—someone fun
and witty and charming who could do anything
she pleased and succeed.

The light in J.D.'s eyes proved her feelings to be
true, and that spurred her on to even more outrageous behavior. At least outrageous for her.

When he didn't pick up his spare, he had to
kiss her.

When she didn't pick up her spare, she had to
kiss him.

When he got two strikes in a row, they had to
dance a slow dance together.

By the time they completed two games, a
waiter made it to the table with a full cart of
silver-covered platters. With a grin, the young
man slipped them onto the table and uncovered
one dish at a time.

Plump, juicy hot dogs, cheese fries still steam-
ing from the fryer, and all the condiments including sauerkraut, freshly cut tomatoes, onions, and
olives were placed in the center of the table.

"I thought you'd enjoy making your own."

"I love it!" Her delightful smile was his answer.

They ate, sometimes feeding themselves, sometimes feeding each other, but always laughing.

"You actually like ketchup and mustard and
mayonnaise?"

The gleam in her eyes kept him mesmerized.

"Why not? I've never tried it all together before, but I like each of them separately."

"Of course," he said dryly. "Why not?"

She lifted up her hot dog. "Open," she ordered.

He did, then took a bite. She watched his white teeth bite into the meat, her heart beating quickly. A speck of mustard caught in the corner of his mouth.

"Wait," she said huskily and leaned forward. Her tongue licked the last of it away.

A moan echoed through his broad chest. Theresa's smile resembled a cat with a fresh pitcher of cream. "You left some."

"You tease too much, woman." His words were a gauntlet.

"Yes."

"You know the price." It was a statement, and from the gleam in his eyes, she knew he'd waited as long as he could.

"I know the price," she repeated huskily. "I set it."

His deep chuckle ran over her nerves like chilled water, making her shake inside with reaction to the thought.

"Yes, but are you ready to pay up?"

"Try me," she stated with more bravado than she felt.

Suddenly, silence reigned. J.D.'s smile melted away, to be replaced with such a look of hunger that it took her breath away. A small voice in the back of her mind told her what she needed to do.

She was the one who made him feel starved for her. *She* was the one he wanted. *She* was the one he needed right now. It gave her a sense of power, but she also felt his need as strongly as she felt her own.

"Where?" Her voice was a bare whisper.

"My office," he said, his voice even softer than hers.

With careful consideration, Theresa placed her half-eaten hot dog on the tray and reached for his hand.

"Lead the way."

J.D. wasted no time. His fingers entwined with hers, and they both walked out the way they'd come in. Then he took a turn, led her through two more rooms and behind a bar. Flipping a key out, he unlocked the door and stood back, allowing her to enter first. But he did not let go of her hand, and she was glad. She needed the contact with him in order to go through with this. She felt daring and decadent and . . . scared.

The office was more like an apartment than a work place. At one end of the room was an enormous rosewood desk with a matching credenza behind it. Papers were neatly piled along the side of the desk, proof that work was accomplished here. The other half of the room was a sitting area with two couches and two wingbacks framing the fireplace, all done in Moroccan reds and forest-greens with a matching Oriental rug. In one corner of the room was a circular staircase leading up to what was a loft over the office area.

"It's beautiful."

"And completely private."

"Do you live here?" she asked, suddenly feeling shy when he closed the door.

His smile was rueful. "I might as well. That's why there's a bedroom upstairs." He nodded toward the metal staircase.

She stared at it until her mouth went dry. *What happens now?* she wondered, panic fringing her thoughts. Did she continue this farce and pretend she was the experienced one, leading him up there? Did she tell him she didn't have the slightest idea how to go about seducing him? Or did she just call the whole thing off?

He guessed her thoughts. "Getting cold feet, Theresa? I wouldn't have imagined a woman as sophisticated as you would try to back out at this stage of the game."

Her eyes sparked with determination. "I wasn't backing out. I was deciding the next course of action."

His brows rose, but she saw the light of mischief in his gaze. "We could go upstairs while you decide. That way we'd be ready for whatever comes next."

Without another word, she walked toward the stairs. His hand still held hers, and he followed as docilely as a lamb to slaughter. But Theresa knew better. J.D. might *look* like an innocent, but he was no more innocent than a vemenous snake. If her

151

own shattered nerves were anything to go by, he was twice as deadly.

They reached the top and she stopped again. A king-sized bed took up most of the room, its lush comforter and stacked pillows in the same colors as the decor downstairs.

Before she could comment, he turned her around to face him. "Come here," he said, his voice a low growl. "I've waited too long to hold you. Now my waiting is over."

His mouth covered hers in a possessive kiss that spoke of feelings long held in check and only now allowed to break free. She was swamped with the emotions he finally displayed. His arms encircled her waist, pulling her as close to the hardness of his body as he could get her. Her hands cradled his head as she kissed him back with all the ardor of a woman caught in the throes of love.

She wanted him as she had never wanted before. She pulled back, her eyes locking with his. Her fingers fumbled with the buttons of her blouse, telling him she was ready for him to do the same.

He did.

Within seconds, they were stripped, and J.D. swung her in his arms, laying her on the thick comforter. Pillows were pushed off the bed as he came down beside her.

His breath was ragged, his throat tight. "My God, I didn't expect you to be so beautiful to look at."

Her laugh was born of nerves. "I'm not. I have stretch marks and—"

"You're beautiful," he stated again, his mouth following a trail from her chin to her breasts, the heat of his kisses counterpointing the cool air blowing silently down on them from the air vents.

Once more her hands played with his neck and hair. When his tongue played with one nipple, it hardened for him and she moaned aloud at the delicious feelings he aroused.

"Ummm, so nice," he muttered before testing the other breast. Her breathing was erratic. Once he'd sampled enough, he took her breast into his mouth. Her breath caught in her throat and she unknowingly arched in delight.

"Tell me what you like," he muttered, but she shook her head in answer. She couldn't put into words what she wanted. She wasn't that experienced or that knowledgeable or brave.

But he wouldn't take no for an answer. "Tell me," he demanded. "Do you like this?" He kissed the underside of her breast.

"Yes."

"Do you like this?" he repeated, teasing her nipple with his tongue.

"Yes."

"What about this?" he questioned, taking the whole breast into his mouth once more and pulling on it.

She arched her back again to give him full access. "Yes!"

His hand cupped the mound between her thighs, his fingers resting right at her now-moist entrance. "And this? Do you like this?"

"Yes."

He slipped his fingers inside the folds, moving back and forth very gently. "And this?" His breath was a rasp, a whisper that worked like sandpaper on her already-raw nerves.

Her moan was his answer.

J.D. gave a rough chuckle, but it ended on his own moan as her hand sought and found his hardness. Her fingers curled around him, matching his rhythm as he touched her.

Magic surrounded them, acting like a lover's cocoon and wrapping them in a sensuous blanket of love. One sensation overlapped another, then another as he found her pleasure spots. He seemed to know when she couldn't take anymore and slowed down to watch her hunger grow again. She tried—she honestly tried to hold on to her sanity. But she couldn't, and she didn't.

Her cries of ecstasy were muffled by his mouth. She held fast to his broad shoulders, feeling as if she were falling off the edge of the earth. Then she floated back into his·arms on a pink cloud. Her breath slowed, her heartbeat slowing, too.

Her lashes fluttered, then opened to stare up at him. His smile was warm and tender and just a little triumphant. She felt a blush creep up her cheeks.

"You were beautiful."

His hand was still protecting her, fingers still gently moving back and forth as if to reassure her that she had really experienced this with him. His mouth was just inches from her parted lips.

"Thank you." It wasn't because of his comment. It was because of her satisfaction.

He understood and smiled, crinkling his eyes in the corners. "You're welcome."

She touched his cheek with a fingernail, outlining a laugh crease. "What can I do? What do you like?" she asked.

His brows raised. "Need you ask? I want to be where you were. I want you to be with me."

"Then why—"

"Because I wanted you to be ready for me, darling. I wanted to watch you and have you know that it was me who took you there. No one else. Just me."

She relaxed again. "It was you," she confirmed.

His mouth touched hers, then sipped at her chin, her neck, the top of her breasts. "I love the taste of your skin," he murmured, nipping until he reached one budding nipple. "I love the taste of you."

Once more she arched her back to accommodate his touch. She didn't want this moment to end. This lethargy was laced with still another need. A need to satisfy as well as be satisfied again. J.D. was an addiction, which she could never get enough of.

Every move, every touch was erotic, sensuous,

and loving. But this time she was also busy, teasing him with her fingers and tongue and lips which never stopped satisfying. His own sighs and sounds egged her on, his own pleas teasing her into new heights of awareness. Soon, he had her climbing that same steep hill, breathless and out of control. But this time, he was with her. When she tugged at his shoulders, he parted her legs and slid between, his desire as obvious as hers. When she set the rhythm, he followed, knowing it was right for both of them.

And when he cried out in ecstasy, she covered his cries with her own.

Chapter Five

With J.D.'s head resting on her breast, Theresa stroked his hair and neck. His latent strength rippled under her hands every time he moved. His mouth puckered, kissing the cleft between her breasts, his warm breath another sweet caress.

She closed her eyes, reveling in the feelings of completeness that filled her body. Ever since the divorce, she'd been afraid to get into a relationship. She'd imagined that she'd buried her sensuality so deep, it would never return or be resurrected. She was wrong. So very wrong. J.D. had just given her back her sense of femininity. It had been in hiding, not dead after all. She had been waiting for the right man to come along. She grinned. Never in a million years would she have guessed it would be *this* man!

J.D. raised his head and stared deeply into her

eyes. "I want you again."

She smiled slowly. A part of him was still buried deep within her. "I know."

"Will this ever stop?"

"Eventually."

"I doubt it."

She didn't know what to say. Her emotions were topsy-turvy. He must have seen her confusion, for he kissed the tip of her nose and laid his head back on her breast, giving her a moment's respite from his gaze.

"Do you remember sneaking out of your house one night and going into your parents' backyard?"

Theresa nodded. Ever since seeing J.D. again, she'd dredged up every memory of him she possessed, then held it, examined it as if she were a microscope and held it as if it were a jewel.

"You wore a sweatshirt that came to your knees. You looked as if you had succeeded at getting out, but you didn't know what to do next."

Theresa's brow cleared. "Yes! You walked along the fence and saw me! Then you got your Monopoly game and we played until almost dawn."

He chuckled. "I had to go to work the next morning and could hardly keep my eyes open. But you had a whole day to sleep."

"You won, if I remember correctly." It was a teasing accusation.

"Yes. And you won my heart. Again," he stated, kissing her shoulder. "I thought it was the luckiest evening of my life."

"Why?"

"Because you noticed me."

At the time it had been wonderful. In fact, the easy yet sensual camaraderie that existed between them that night was what had given her the courage to ask him out. She had felt so relaxed and carefree, and most of all, protected. It had never been that way with . . .

"I always noticed you, I was just too young to know what I wanted. I was a fool."

He kissed her again. "So was I. I let you go."

"You had no choice," she stated wryly. "I was bound and determined to screw up with the boy of my nightmares."

"I should have insisted you give me a chance. I should have declared you were mine instead of letting you leave the dance with Charlie."

Her arms tightened around his shoulders. She stared at the ceiling. What would have happened if he had pursued her? Would she have been swayed? Would they have gotten married? Longing for what might have been washed over her, bringing tears to her eyes with the pain of it. Could happiness be that close and still not attained? One decision had changed her whole life path. One wrong decision. . . .

"Don't." He spoke low, with a gruff rasp that told her he had thought the same thing. "It doesn't matter now. We're together."

He moved inside her and her body reacted instantly.

"I was so dumb," she said in a whisper, still suspended between yesterday and today.

"You were a child. Too young to be ready for the kind of commitment I want from you now, Theresa. So was I."

He rocked into her and she rocked back slowly and easily, as if it were the most natural motion in the world. It felt as if they had been together a thousand times before and knew how to move to please both each other and themselves.

Theresa closed her eyes to hide from the intensity of his gaze. Then she was transported to a time and place where only the two of them could go.

Heat flowed through her body like a rocket. Her eyes flew open and, for one shining moment, she dissolved inside the warm, blue eyes of J.D. Trainer.

Theresa barely made it to work on time. Everything she did that night was done by rote and yet she'd never sounded so good. She teased the customers, played by ear several pieces of music she didn't know, and laughed at every little joke.

She felt great!

Although she kept her eye on the door, J.D. did not show up that night. But her excitement of the afternoon kept her from feeling the dark disappointment of the evening. After all, she told herself, he had a business to run. Besides, she was to meet him again tomorrow for lunch.

Every time she closed her eyes for a moment,

she saw the image of a naked J.D. making love to her, kissing her, languishing in the aftermath of their lovemaking. God! It had felt so very wonderful to be held again. She had forgotten the closeness that only sharing can bring.

Tomorrow for lunch was her battle cry for the rest of the evening.

With such a magical promise dangling in front of her, it was a miracle she slept at all.

But she did.

J.D. stood in the middle of the busy, customer-crowded arcade, pretending he was surveying the area. His employees were on their best behavior because they thought he was watching. He wasn't.

No matter how hard he tried, he couldn't seem to erase Theresa from his mind. Everywhere he turned, her image overlaid whatever was in front of him. Her body was lithe and supple, leaning over him as if ready to grant him anything his heart desired. He could even see his dark hand on the white of her thigh and remember the softness of her skin, the texture of her nipple as he leaned forward to taste it. The warm silkiness of being inside her was one of heaven's greatest gifts.

Someone laughed loudly and he started, realizing he'd just done it again. In the middle of a crowd he had lost himself to a memory. Worse, he was standing in front of his employees and customers with a need that was making itself all too evident.

He gave up trying to work the floor this evening. His employees could take care of themselves, he decided as he walked back toward his office. He wasn't going to step out of the office again tonight or tomorrow. Not until Theresa arrived.

A smile formed his lips. Theresa had finally *seen* him. Oh, not as the big guy who sat behind her on the bus, or as the guy who could make her jerk of a boyfriend jealous. Theresa didn't even see him as the owner of a successful club. She saw the man— John Trainer who loved deeply, laughed hard and enjoyed all phases of life. He knew that was what she saw because, after making love twice, they'd lain in each other's arms and talked and talked. It wasn't until it was almost time for her to leave that they made love again.

And she had been everything he'd imagined her to be: witty, warm, and real. Not filled with ideas of life that weren't based in reality. She wasn't looking for a man to take care of her and protect her for the rest of her life while she spent his money. She was looking for a helpmate, some-one to share her life with. Theresa was looking for the same thing he was: someone to give love to.

Undoing his tie, he walked up the stairs to the loft. He slipped out of his tuxedo and threw it on the chair, then climbed between sheets that were still scented with Theresa. His arms behind his back, he stared at the ceiling as if it were a giant screen TV.

A frown formed between his brows. Even though she had shared and laughed and loved, J.D. still felt there was a reserve about her. Some little wall he couldn't see and couldn't knock down. He didn't know what it was, but until he could find it and break through it, he doubted Theresa would commit to marriage.

He didn't know *how* he knew this, he just *knew*.

Determination etched his strong features as he glared at the ceiling. Tomorrow, he'd take care of that last wall. By the first week of February, he wanted Theresa to say yes to his marriage proposal. That gave him one week. . . .

The next week was one of the most magical Theresa had ever experienced. Every day J.D. planned something different. They had a gunfight in the video corral, then ate barbecue for lunch. They played electronic golf, then shared a picnic minus the ants. They made a video of the two of them singing "Feelings," complete with a backdrop out of MTV. Then they ate junk food, having a food fight with the potato chips. J.D. even surprised her with several games of blackjack, while plying her with nonalcoholic drinks. Steak, potatoes, and fresh vegetables were the order of that day.

Every day ended in his office, then his bedroom, making love until they were sated—for the moment. Every day left Theresa feeling as if she had been given a second chance.

She was a teenager again, and she loved it.

When she woke up in the morning, there was a gleam in her eye and a smile on her lips that hadn't been there for many, many years.

But there was also guilt. If she had been older when she'd married Charlie, would they have had a better chance of making their marriage work? Had her marriage failed because *she'd* failed as a wife?

Thank goodness it was Saturday night and she and J.D. had a date for tonight. She could forget her guilt while she was with him. This time they were leaving the club and going somewhere else. She didn't know where. It was to be a surprise. And Sunday they had plans for a drive in the country.

Every chance he got, J.D. told her he loved her. It was wonderful to hear, and she was greedy, wanting him to say it as often as he could. But still she worried. When the newness of love wore off, would J.D. tire of her?

No. This time would be different, she told herself. This time was forever. So why did her heart feel as if this relationship was too good to last? She refused to answer that question.

The exclusive restaurant was located on the banks of Buffalo Bayou, one of the main water arteries that had helped make Houston into the city it now was. The entire back of the restaurant was glass from floor to ceiling, creating lovely views no matter which way the customer turned. Although the trees were first-of-February bare, most of the bushes and grass hadn't died and shadings of green still stubbornly clung to the hillside. Well-manicured plants and ivy abounded, separating each table from the other and giving a feeling of privacy.

J.D. touched the small of Theresa's back as they followed the waitress toward one of the cozy tables by the window. Suddenly, someone grabbed her arm. Startled, she looked down— and into the leering expression of her ex-husband. Sitting next to him was a very pregnant young woman whose face showed her own embarrassment. Obviously, Charlie's new wife recognized her.

Theresa's face must have shown her surprise.

"Well, well, Theresa. So you finally found someone to take you out. Congratulations."

"Charlie," she began in a low voice, wondering how she could avoid a scene. He was in one of his nasty moods and judging from the grip on her arm, he wasn't about to let the opportunity pass.

"Did you tell him you weren't capable of passion? Or will he find out the hard way, huh?"

From behind Theresa, J.D. looked over her shoulder. "Good evening, Charlie. It looks like you haven't changed since you were a teenager. You're still a punk."

Charlie's face went from white to a deep red. "John Trainer."

"How nice of you to remember." J.D.'s voice was as dry as brittle winter leaves.

"You were a bully then, too." Charlie's mouth pulled into a sneer, but Theresa knew he'd lost his equilibrium. "Don't tell me you finally got the girl of your dreams. Are you sure you know what to do with her, Big John?"

"Obviously better than you did. You were stupid enough to lose her." J.D. nodded toward the woman sitting across from Charlie. "Sorry you had to witness this, ma'am. We'll leave you to enjoy the remainder of your dinner."

With his hand on her elbow, J.D. led a shaking Theresa to their table. A nervous waitress laid menus on their plates and disappeared into the hostess area.

Theresa sat down and stared at the menu in front of her. She clasped her hands in her lap, her fingers twined into a tight knot. Her breathing was shallow, short, and she purposely took a deep breath.

"It's all right, Theresa," J.D. said in a low voice. "He's leaving now."

She looked up at J.D., her brown eyes wide and hurt. He wished he could erase the last few minutes from her memory. He wished he could hold her and tell her how wonderful she was and what a sad no-good son of a . . .

"It doesn't matter," Theresa said in a low voice. "I think it was necessary to meet him sometime. If for no other reason then to remember how little we had in common." She shook her head back and forth. "What a terrible mistake I made. How could I have believed that he loved me?"

J.D. leaned forward. "Because he said so, and you were young. You were just a kid, Theresa. So was he. You weren't old enough to know what the signs were, so you took him at face value. It happens all the time."

"But I still chose him, J.D. I still chose that way of life. In fact, I stayed with him even after I knew our marriage was over."

"Many people do, honey. It's hard to find the courage to end it."

"I should have been able to make it work. If I had . . ." She stared at him, finally her dry eyes filled with tears. She blinked, refusing to allow them to fall. "I might have been able to salvage our marriage if I had tried harder."

"Theresa," J.D. stared at her. How could she want a jerk who had just done what he had done? How could she even *think* of trying to salvage something out of a relationship that had harmed her so? Knowing Charlie, J.D. would bet he'd never worried about trying to save their marriage. It wasn't something that would give a public return on his investment. If what he wanted didn't come to him easily, he got angry. Anger was his answer to everything, even as a teenager. He was still the same selfish bastard he'd always been.

Theresa laid her napkin back on her plate. Tears glistened in her eyes as she stared at him. "I'm sorry, J.D. I really am."

He knew what she was going to say and his heart dropped to his stomach. "Theresa. Don't."

"This won't work. You know that. You're wonderful, J.D. You deserve . . ." She stood. "I'm sorry."

"He knew what buttons to push, Theresa. Don't let him succeed. Don't let him *win*."

"I . . . I'm sorry."

With staccato steps, she walked through the maze of tables to the entrance. J.D. sat completely still, his eyes glued to the woman he loved as he watched her leave. There was no use following her. Something in her eyes told him that she'd made up her mind about them. Until he knew how she came to that conclusion, he couldn't fight it.

It took everything he had to force himself to remain in his chair. Everything he'd worked toward, dreamed of, and believed in had just walked out of his life. But he'd get her back. He swore it.

Later, when she was calmer, he would question her about what was going on in that mind of hers. He could combat anything once he knew what it was.

But, right now, all he could do was watch his

own dreams go up in a puff of smoke.
Damn youth.
Damn his own stupid thoughts back then.
Damn that stupid Charlie for tonight.

Chapter Six

Theresa popped open the cork on the wine bottle and poured herself a glass of her finest. This was a night to celebrate. She glanced at the clock, noting it was two in the morning. Okay, so it was a morning to celebrate.

She had just realized how scared of making the same mistake *twice* she really was.

All the nonfiction self-help books would call this a breakthrough. She called it frightening knowledge.

Had she chosen J.D. to fall in love with? Was she choosing a man who, although he didn't look or act like Charlie, would show those same self-ish tendencies, the same self-absorption that had allowed Charlie to ignore her for days, sometimes weeks?

Tears kept streaming down her cheeks, but she ignored them as she walked into her small living room. Tears had been a part of her life for so long that she was immune to them. Sitting in the large wingback chair, Theresa relived the scene with Charlie and his new wife.

J.D. was as brutal as Charlie had been. Did that mean they had something in common? When she made love with J.D., he controlled the situation. When they ate, it was his choice what the food would be.

No, her conscience proclaimed. That wasn't fair. J.D. had chosen their menus because it was his restaurant and he had to order ahead of time for the chefs to get it ready. And if he hadn't taken charge of their lovemaking, she might never have made the overture. Until J.D. came along, she had not been encouraged to be the aggressor. In fact, touching was a taboo unless it was done in the dark of night. Not so with J.D. He stroked her all the time, and she found that the more he gave her the more she craved. She'd turned into a greedy child, needing as much as he could give.

The funny thing was that he didn't seem to mind at all. In fact, Theresa was sure that J.D. loved touching and stroking her as much as she loved being the recipient.

Amazing.

But the fact remained. Staying with J.D. was too scary to bear. She couldn't do it anymore.

He would expect more from her as time went on and she couldn't give it, wasn't capable of giving it. His attitude toward her would change as they got to know each other, and she couldn't stand to see that change. No. Better to have the memories of the past four weeks to cherish than to watch everything, including her dreams, deteriorate.

It was over.

It was best.

It was lonely.

The rest of her life stretched in front of her like a long, narrow road. It looked lonely and barren, but it was her own choice.

Theresa sipped her wine and continued to stare into the fireplace.

"Welcome to the rest of my life," she murmured aloud. Then Theresa closed her eyes and relived every moment of her time with J.D.

"But if you were so wonderful together, why would you break it off?" Gayle asked, her brow wrinkled in perplexity. "Most people don't run away from happiness, Theresa. They *strive* for it."

"I can't take the chance of making the same mistake twice." Theresa tried to swallow the lump in her throat. "Don't you see? If I make a mistake and get involved with someone like Charlie again, I'll *never* recuperate! Look how long it took me to recover from my marriage, Gayle! Despite the fact that I no longer loved Charlie at the end, I felt that we were a team, a pair. When I left, I thought I'd never get over Charlie. But if it happened again . . ."

Gayle's eyes were wide with disbelief. "Are you telling me you believe that Charlie and J.D. are the same type of man?"

"I don't know."

"Well, I can tell you that they aren't. No way," her friend stated emphatically. "And how you could say they are is beyond me."

"Because it's true. J.D. is just as opinionated and single-minded as Charlie is. And J.D. has a temper. I saw it the other night. He could slice through a person's ego like a warm knife through butter."

Gayle looked patiently at her friend. "Theresa, no man—or woman—gets to be successful without knowing how to be ruthless on occasion."

"I know."

"And no one will be a hundred percent nice and sweet."

"I know."

"And everyone on earth, whether they express it or not, has some kind of opinion on something."

"I know."

"So those things are held to be common in all people—even females, right?" Gayle persisted.

"Yes, but . . ." Theresa began.

"No, that's just the way it is. J.D. also happens

to have two legs, two arms, two ears, and two eyes. Just because Charlie has the same inventory, you won't hold that against J.D., too, will you?"

"Don't get smart," Theresa said, a wry smile barely tilting her lips up. "I understand what you're saying, but it's been proven that women choose the same type of man time and time again, making themselves miserable in the process."

Gayle placed her coffee mug in front of her and held it with both hands, her frown returning. "You're saying that if you had chosen J.D. at the Valentine's dance when we were teenagers, you might have wound up in the same spot as you are now—divorced and alone while heading into middle age."

Theresa nodded miserably. "Exactly." Then, her eyes widened. "How did you know about the Valentine's dance?"

Gayle smiled. "J.D. told me a little about it. I figured you didn't want to talk about it, but I know enough to imagine what both of you went through."

"And to think that I could have had the same marriage with a different man is a very real thing."

Gayle sighed. "Well, friend. I can't help you there. You might be right. Who knows how we grow up and what paths we might have taken if we'd been with someone else? I don't know where I would have been if I had chosen someone other than Pierce to marry."

Theresa grinned despite herself. "Pierce chose you, you nut. He chased you all over town until you finally gave in and gave up."

Gayle grinned back. "True, but it was my choice. I had to wait until he could see the wisdom of his ways and then think that it was his decision."

Theresa leaned back. "You were always good at getting what you want, Gayle. When you wanted something, you never sat back and waited for it to come to you. You went after it. Don't you see, I was never like that. And now, I'm not even sure *what* I want, let alone how to go after it."

"You want J.D.," her friend confirmed.

"Yes. But is he good for me?" Theresa stared down at her hands resting on the table. She'd never felt so miserable or so confused. There was no answer in sight.

"Yes."

"How do you know?"

"Because you're miserable now."

"I could be even more miserable, Gayle. I can't take that chance. I've only now gotten my life together."

Gayle stood and sighed. "Okay, Theresa. Whatever you say. I can't *make* you see what you're missing. Only you can do that." She carried her cup to the sink and rinsed it out. "All I can say is that I'm here for you if you need me."

Theresa stood and walked over to Gayle, giving her a hug. "Thanks, friend."

It was reassuring to know that Gayle might

not always agree with her, but their friendship wouldn't suffer because of it.

After Gayle's departure, she walked around the house, touching a chair, brushing fingers over a statue. When she'd left her husband, she'd left everything else behind, too. Her townhouse was furnished with all new things. There was nothing to remind her of those unhappy years. Nothing but sad memories.

Her next thought was that if she could slide by Valentine's Day without seeing J.D. or reliving every memory of that fateful dance, she could make it through anything. After all, she was tough, she was strong, she was woman—alone. That thought was not comforting, but it was realistic.

Even though Valentine's Day wasn't until to-morrow, the room was decorated with hearts and flowers. J.D. stared around the private dining area, satisfied with the results. Usually seating no more than thirty people, the area was now only ready for two.

Ever since talking to Gayle and gleaning a part of the problem, he'd been planning this *tête à tête*. Now, on to the next step.

He picked up the telephone and dialed Theresa's number. When she answered, he heard the sadness in her voice. It matched the sadness in his own soul.

"Hi, Theresa. It's J.D. I have a few personal

items you left here and I need you to pick them up today."

"I . . ."—she cleared her throat—"I'll have to do that tomorrow, J.D. I'm sorry."

"I need it done today, Theresa," he stated firmly, hoping he could push this issue enough to convince her. With Gayle's help, she should agree. "I'm leaving town tonight and won't be back for quite a while."

"I see," she said slowly, and then J.D. heard Gayle's whispered voice in the background. "Okay, J.D. Gayle and I will be by to pick it up this afternoon. Any special time?"

"Any time before four," he said quickly.

When she agreed, he hung up and grinned. So far, so good. He prayed everything would go as he had planned.

Theresa's hand hesitated on the door leading into J.D.'s club. When she visited here she had always imagined herself transported in time back to her youth. J.D. had made her feel that way, and that was part of the problem. She shook her head, telling herself to stop being so fanciful. She was picking up a bracelet and earrings from a man she once dated. That was all.

Gayle prodded her. "Well? Are we going in?"

"Of course," Theresa said, opening the portals. Gayle silently followed.

Every other time she'd ever come to the Magic Time Machine J.D. had been at the entrance of the front dining area to meet her. She was surprised at her own disappointment.

This time, there was a young waiter. "Ma'am? Mr. Trainer is waiting in one of the rooms. Please follow me," he said.

At her nod, he turned and led the way.

Several of the rooms they went through brought back instant-replay memories, and they were all of J.D. Tension knotted Theresa's every nerve. She wanted to run, and the only reason she continued to follow the young waiter was that Gayle was directly behind her. If she ran away right now, Gayle would never forget. Theresa didn't think she wanted to live with Gayle's disapproval or disappointment.

Stopping in front of a closed door, the young man knocked.

"Just a minute," J.D. called, and the waiter grinned.

"He'll be right out," the waiter reassured her, and Theresa nodded in understanding.

"To our knowledge," Gayle teased in a whisper, "J.D. has tested negative for rabies. I don't think he'll bite."

"Smart aleck," Theresa answered in a shaky voice.

But her friend had helped bring into perspective the expectation of seeing J.D. again. Whatever happened, she knew that J.D. would not hurt her. At least not intentionally.

"Come in," J.D. called.

Rita Clay Estrada

Theresa stiffened, fear running down her spine. She wanted to see him so much, it hurt. She wanted to run away even more. Indecision was etched on her face as she stood in front of the door.

"Go ahead," Gayle urged, giving her a light push.

She couldn't think of an excuse not to do as Gayle said. Theresa opened the door and walked in. She didn't hear the door close behind her. She didn't see J.D. standing by the juke box. She didn't see anything but the Valentine red-and-white decorations.

The room was decorated in crepe paper, balloons, posterboard hearts, and other frills. It was their high-school Valentine's Day dance all over again.

A slow melody drifted through the room and Theresa turned toward the juke box—and J.D. The ballad wrapped around them as the Beatles soulfully sang.

His full mouth held a tender smile that touched her heart. She watched him walk toward her, stopping only when he was inches away. She couldn't move. She couldn't speak. There was a lump in her throat as large as the record on the turntable.

J.D. placed a silvery cardboard tiara on her head. "I believe this belongs to you," he murmured, then kissed her forehead.

Once more, she was transported back in time, experiencing the feelings of a high-school girl. But

180

this time there was a slight difference. Something she wasn't sure of but felt as deeply as if it were a part of her. She had a second chance.

As if in slow motion, J.D. wrapped his arms around her waist, bringing her close to his hips.

Then, just as they had twenty years ago, they moved around the dance floor, cocooned in each other's arms as the same music wove its magic around them.

Theresa rested her head on his shoulder, her arms around his waist, just as his were around hers.

"I wasn't the Sweetheart," she finally protested.

"You are this time," was his answer. The sound vibrated through his chest, reassuring her that this wasn't a dream.

"And you?" she asked, reluctantly drawing back to see his face. "Are you the Prince?"

"Make no mistake, Theresa. I'm *your* prince."

She opened her mouth to dispute that, only to close it again. She smiled before he pulled her back into his arms and they continued to dance.

One lingering song led to another, but their dancing slowed until they barely moved. She felt every muscle of his body against hers. His cologne mingled with his own personal scent and filled her senses. Even the cut of his tuxedo seemed to be out of her fantasy era.

"It's twenty years ago," he whispered in her ear. "We're at the Valentine's Day dance at school. We've got a second chance, Theresa. Charlie's ghost and I are waiting for your decision. Are you going to leave me and choose Charlie again? Do we have to live through all those mistakes this time? Or are you going to choose me?"

She swallowed hard, knowing he was asking for a commitment that she wasn't sure she could make. She had never yearned for anything as much as a second chance with J.D. Trainer. But the practical side of her knew what the chances for happiness were.

"No matter who I choose, I could be making the same mistake, John. It could be me who has the problem. Not you. Not Charlie."

"If that's the case, darlin', then you're halfway through not making that mistake again. Once you recognize it, it's no longer the big error." He kissed the side of her cheek. "Don't use yourself as an excuse to lose out on happiness again."

The music shifted into another of her favorite Beatles' songs, "Yesterday." J.D.'s hands tightened slightly on her hips, reminding her of his touch when they made love. She ached for the way his fingers grazed her breasts, her thighs. . . .

"Theresa. You've got the chance to make a different choice. We both do."

She drew a shaky breath. "I'm scared."

"I know. So am I."

She raised a hand and let her fingers follow his jaw line. "What do you want from me, J.D.? What do you expect from all this?"

He sighed, closing his eyes. When he opened them again, his blue gaze delved deep inside her, showing her a vulnerable side of him she'd never seen before. Her heart wanted to wrap around him, to protect him from her own ability to hurt him. But she couldn't. Instead, standing on tiptoes, she dropped a light as a butterfly kiss on his cheek.

Now it was her turn to prompt. "Tell me. Tell me what you want."

"I want you by my side. I want us to go through the rest of our lives together. I want to cry with you, laugh with you, make love with you at all times of the day or night. Occasionally, I even want to fight with you. I want to share your ups and downs, and share mine with you. I want total commitment."

He held her close, smelling the light scent of her hair. "I want you. All of you. I won't settle for less."

"What if I can't give you that?"

"You can." His voice was sure and strong.

"J.D., I . . ."

The record ended and he stopped dancing. Taking a step back, he stared down at her. "I'm not Charlie. You're not the young girl who chose the devil she knew over the devil she didn't know all those years ago. You have a second wish. Use it, Theresa."

Another Beatles song came on, one fraught with

memories. "I Need You" was a song she used to think meant Charlie. Now J.D. was infusing the tune with other memories. For as long as she lived, Theresa didn't think she'd ever forget the image of J.D. standing on the dance floor as she walked off with young Charlie. At the time, he hadn't looked hurt or scared or even young. But now she knew better. J.D. had hurt more than she had ever dreamed. Almost as much as she had yearned for a second chance all those years ago.

And now, here he was, putting himself on the line for more hurt while giving her a second chance.

"I love you," she whispered.

"I know," he said quietly. "But how much?"

"Enough to feel as if you're a part of my world. That I'm being absorbed into a part of yours."

"Enough to marry me?"

"Enough to marry you."

He closed his eyes. "Thank God."

"Oh, J.D.," she said, sighing, tightening her arms around his waist. "For both our sakes, I hope I know what I'm doing."

"You do." He chuckled huskily. "Tomorrow, we're flying to Mexico and getting married on an island in the sun. But, until then, I'm not letting you out of my sight."

"Happy Valentine's Day, love," she whispered.

"Happy Valentine's Day, with a thousand more to come, Tess. They'll last as long as I'm alive to give them to you," he promised before claiming her lips in a searing kiss.

Theresa didn't hear the music anymore. J.D.'s words were music to her ears.

BRANSON'S DAUGHTER
Lynda Trent

Chapter One

Hannah Branson shifted her suitcase to her other hand as she climbed the familiar, worn cement steps. A breeze, unseasonably warm for February, lifted the hem of her skirt and ruffled her auburn hair. She hesitated on the small porch, reminded of the colors it had been over the years by the peeling layers of paint. She had lived in this house the first eighteen years of her life, but even though she had many memories of that time, it all seemed oddly foreign to her now. Every time she came back for a visit, she was reminded of the truth in the adage that you can't go home again.

Feeling awkward doing so, Hannah pushed the doorbell button. Hearing no responding chime, she knocked. A few moments later, the door was opened, cautiously at first, then wider as her mother recognized her.

"Hannah! What are you doing, knocking at your own house?" Leah Branson pushed open the screen door, allowing her daughter to enter.

"It's not really my house anymore, Mama. I've lived away almost half of my life."

"Nonsense. As long as there's breath in my body, this will always be your home." Leah stepped back and gazed at her daughter. "You sure turned out pretty, Hannah. You did for a fact."

With a shy smile Hannah had thought she had outgrown, she put her suitcase on the floor. "Thanks, Mama. You're looking well."

Leah laughed and smoothed her work-reddened hands over the cotton print of her dress and the old shapeless cardigan she wore against the drafts. "You'd be the one to know if anyone did. Imagine you, a doctor!"

Hannah smiled at the pride in her mother's voice and looked around the room. It hadn't changed since her last visit nor in the fifteen years she had been gone, but it seemed somewhat smaller, darker. "I wish you'd let me buy you a bigger house. One in a nicer neighborhood."

"Don't be silly. Why, you know I've lived here ever since your daddy and I married. This is my home. There's nothing wrong with this place."

"I noticed the junked cars on the corner lot down the street and most of the houses around you are in need of paint and repairs. Clearwater may be a small town, but that doesn't mean there's no crime."

"Land's sake," Leah said in a dismissive voice. "Let me fix you some coffee. I've got a pot brewing."

Hannah followed her mother into the small kitchen. Like the rest of the house, it was spotless, though it bore the evidence of years of living. The red-speckled linoleum was darker in the middle of the room where traffic had worn away the colored layer, and the top coat of paint on the cabinet doors had been scrubbed so often the color beneath was showing through in places. The counter top was small, cramped, and worn down to its black subsurface in several spots. The smell of coffee, an aroma Hannah always associated with her mother, filled the room.

Leah got two coffee mugs from the cabinet next to the sink, and as she filled them, she said, "I guess you're looking forward to the class reunion."

"In a way I am." Hannah took the cup offered her and sat at the formica table. "It's been fifteen years since I graduated from high school. Everyone will have changed."

"I'll bet none have changed as much as you have."

"No, I doubt anyone has."

Leah sat opposite Hannah. "It's been a long time, Hannah. I've missed you."

Hannah felt a stab of guilt. "I should have been back more often, Mama. I feel bad about that."

"That's okay, baby. I understand." Leah reached out and covered Hannah's hand.

"Where is he?"

Leah pulled her hand back and sighed. "I look for him to come in any minute." Brightening her tone, she said, "Tell me about yourself. What's it like to live in Austin?"

"It's a far cry from Clearwater." Hannah sipped the scalding black coffee. "I wish you'd come visit me. You've never seen my apartment."

"It's hard for me to get away, what with my work and your daddy being like he is."

"I've made friends, and I stay busy most of the time." She never admitted to her mother that she was often lonesome despite her friends and hectic schedule. At thirty-three her biological clock was ticking loudly, and she wanted a husband and family of her own. Unfortunately, not one of her male friends was a bachelor she was likely to become interested in romantically.

"You always were popular."

"Mama, you know I wasn't. I was too shy to be popular. Half the time I was afraid to so much as speak to a boy."

"You weren't afraid to speak to the McCullough boy."

Hannah had dreaded this moment almost as much as she had looked forward to it. Forcing her voice to sound casual, she asked, "How is Trey?"

"Fine, as far as I know. He still lives here. You

know he married that cheerleader—what was her name? Eve?"

"Eden. Eden Clark." Hannah wasn't likely to forget that name. Eden had boasted to Hannah that she would marry Trey regardless of what it took. They had been married before the summer was out, not two weeks before Hannah was to start college in Arlington.

"I can't keep up with your crowd," Leah admitted. "Seems like everybody's getting divorced and remarrying these days. I don't see how a body keeps his own address straight."

"Trey and Eden are still married, aren't they?" Hannah hated the spark of hope that flared within her that her mother would say it wasn't true.

"Got me. I see him on the street at times, but that's not something that you can ask a person you barely know, and divorce notices aren't printed in the newspaper. I never heard of them having a baby, though." Her blue eyes searched Hannah's face. "You don't still care about him, do you? Not after all these years."

"Of course not," she said as convincingly as she could. "I had all but forgotten his name." It was so blatant a lie she was surprised her mother didn't call her on it. Hannah would never forget a single thing about Trey McCullough.

Hannah heard footsteps on the back porch and her muscles tensed. The kitchen door swung open, and a man with stringy graying hair stepped into the room. He blinked at Hannah as if he wasn't

Lynda Trent

sure he believed his eyes.

"Hello, Papa," Hannah said cautiously.

"I wondered whose fancy car that was out front." Amos Branson swayed in the doorway as he gestured vaguely toward the front of the house. "I thought maybe one of those high-falutin' women from across town was out here hiring your mama to scrub and clean."

Hannah blushed. She felt bad about her mother having to work so hard as a maid, and her father never let her forget it. From the way he spoke, a person who didn't know better would have assumed he and Leah had been the ones to put Hannah through college and medical school, when in fact, not a penny had come from them. "I was just telling Mama that she should let me help out."

Leah gave a nervous laugh. "As if we'd take a dime from our only child."

"I'd take it and welcome it." Amos swayed and put out a hand to steady himself against the counter. "Just give me whatever you feel like donating to the cause."

Hannah could not meet his rheumy eyes. He was drunk already. She had hoped she had been mistaken when he had first started to speak. He had been drunk for so many years his speech was always a bit slurred and uncertain, even on the rare occasions when he was sober.

"I'm surprised to see you. I told Leah you wouldn't show up." Amos fumbled about in

192

the kitchen cabinets until he found a bottle of whiskey. He poured some of the amber liquid into a jelly glass and tossed down a liberal amount.

"I come as often as I can." Hannah tried to keep her voice calm. She was determined not to let him goad her into an argument before she had been in the house half an hour.

"She's real busy," Leah said as if she had inside information. "First there was college classes and then that medical school. Then she had to intern and now she has a practice to keep up. Our Hannah is real busy."

Hannah smiled at her mother. "I'll try to get back more often. Just recently I've found a doctor who is willing to trade off days with me, and that will give me more free time." Guilt again filled her. She could have come home more often, even before having made such an arrangement, and thought her mother must surely know that. But knowing that Trey and Eden lived here together and that she couldn't visit her mother without having to be around her father as well had kept her away. "How about you, Papa? Are you working these days?"

"Nope, can't do it." Amos scratched his gaunt stomach. "My health ain't what it used to be. That old back injury has been acting up something fierce."

"Why not let me take a look at it?" Hannah had heard him complain about his bad back all her life, but she had never known it to stop him from drinking and carousing, only from working. "Maybe I can cure it."

Amos frowned at her. "You're getting sassy these days, ain't you."

"She didn't mean nothing," Leah said quickly. "She was just offering to help."

Amos didn't look convinced. "It was a mistake letting you go to college. It put ideas into your head. You always was putting on airs and trying to act better than your mama and me."

Fighting the urge to run from the room, Hannah stood and walked unhurriedly back into the living room to get her suitcase. With her temper barely in check, she passed back through the kitchen on her way to her old bedroom. Unable to resist the temptation, she said, "Women are allowed to think these days, Papa. We've even been allowed the vote."

Leah made a shushing motion as she herded Hannah from the room and in an undertone said, "Don't get him stirred up, honey. He's had a bit to drink."

"When hasn't he?" Hannah whispered back.

"You just remember who you are," Amos roared after them from the kitchen. "This is my house and you're just visiting. Don't you get uppity with me!"

Hannah didn't answer. She put her suitcase on the floor of her room and glanced about. The white chenille bedspread with some of the tufts missing, the bed with its no longer familiar sag in the middle, and the cheap blond furniture that had been discarded by one of Leah's employers many years past were the same as they always had been. "Looks like I'm home again." She tried to smile at her mother. "At least for the week-end."

Across town Trey McCullough sat in his mother's living room and sipped coffee from a delicate china cup. "Why did you want me to stop by?" he asked.

"No reason, really. It's so lonely here now that your father is gone. Especially at dinnertime."

Trey lifted his head and looked at the oil painting of his father hanging over the mantel. Andrew McCullough, the second, had sat for that portrait when he was about the age Trey was now. Trey's resemblance to his father was remarkable. Both had the same pale gold hair that was the McCullough trademark and hazel eyes that could look straight through a person in court. "He's been gone for two years, Mother."

"That doesn't mean I'm not still lonely," she snapped. Then, because she was talking to her son, she softened her voice. "I saw Eden and her mother the other day."

"Oh?" Trey hoped she wouldn't start in on Eden again.

"She's looking more beautiful than ever. She's had her hair lightened to a silvery-blond, and her eyes are as blue as they can be."

Trey smiled. "She wears tinted contacts. Her eyes aren't blue at all."

Ruth McCullough frowned at him with her red lips pursed the same way they always had been when she was trying not to reprimand him. "I still think you ought to call her, especially this weekend."

"Why do you say that?"

"It's your fifteenth class reunion, remember? You are going, aren't you?"

"I don't know. I had planned to, but I'm considering backing out."

"That might be best. After all, you have so little in common with those people these days. Most of you have lost contact with each other, and the ones that stayed in Clearwater see each other all the time. I think class reunions are pointless."

"I thought you were all for me going."

"I was all for you taking Eden. There's a difference. I thought that would give you a reason to call her and ask her out."

"Mother, I don't need a reason to call a woman. And I have no intention of ever calling or dating Eden again, let alone remarrying her."

"I'm so disappointed in you at times. Your father would certainly have had something to say to you about your attitude."

"I'm sure he would have, but Eden and I are divorced, and I like it that way."

"She never got over you, you know. Her mother has told me so on more than one occasion."

"I find that difficult to believe. She's been married twice since then, and neither of those marriages worked out either. That should tell you something about how hard it is to get along with her."

"Nonsense. It's just a matter of setting priorities. Your father and I didn't have a perfectly smooth marriage either. No one does."

Trey didn't reply. He easily recalled how loveless his parents' marriage had been. There had been few arguments, but that was because his parents seldom spoke to each other or went anywhere together. He had wanted more from his own marriage, but that, too, had been a bitter disappointment. For a moment he allowed himself to think about the girl he had dated in high school, Hannah Branson. Would she be at the reunion?

"Have a cucumber sandwich," Ruth said as she held the silver tray toward him. "Bertha made them especially for you."

"I don't like cucumber sandwiches. Father did, not me."

"Nonsense. You've always liked them. You're just being difficult. You'll hurt Bertha's feelings."

Trey took a triangular sandwich, not because his mother insisted, but because he didn't want to upset Bertha. She had worked for the family for as long as Trey could remember, and she always made a peach cobbler, Trey's favorite dessert, when she knew ahead of time that he was coming for dinner.

"There! You see? I told you that you liked them." Ruth took a sandwich and ate it in small bites. "It's such a pity that you and Eden had no children."

"I think it was a blessing. Who'd want to drag children through a messy divorce?"

"It needn't have been messy. It needn't have happened at all."

"Mother, she was seeing another man. They were planning to be married as soon as the divorce was final and the month-long waiting period was up."

"She was only trying to make you jealous. Women do that from time to time. It doesn't mean a thing."

Trey put the half-eaten sandwich on his saucer. "I have to go."

"Don't run off just because I accidentally brought up something you don't want to talk about. You'll have to talk about it if you go to this reunion. I know for a fact Eden is planning to go. She and her mother were shopping for a dress for her to wear to the dance on Saturday."

"If you want me to stay, stop talking about Eden. We're divorced and that's the way it's going to stay."

Ruth sighed as if she found him unreasonable.

"Very well. We won't talk about Eden, even if I do know you're wrong. How was court today?"

"Same as it always is. The man who robbed the convenience store was found guilty, but that was no surprise. He was caught with his hand in the money drawer. The only amazing aspect of that case was that he insisted on a trial at all."

"Your father used to tell me the most wickedly interesting stories about his cases. You never tell me anything at all. The newspaper is more informative."

"It's the newspaper's business to be. I have to respect my clients' privacy. You could come to the trials if you're that interested."

Ruth typically wrinkled her nose, a gesture that had been more appealing before her face had settled into permanent wrinkles. "Can you imagine me in court? It smells of spittoons and sweat socks."

Trey laughed. "Spittoons? There's not a spittoon in the whole building. When was the last time you smelled sweat socks?"

"Anyway, I would be completely out of place there." She gazed up at the portrait of her husband. "I do miss him so. You must feel the same way about Eden, don't you?"

Trey gave her an exasperated glance.

"You can't blame me for wanting the best for you," Ruth objected. "A mother knows what's right for her child."

Lynda Trent

"Your 'child' is thirty-three years old and able to take care of himself."

Ruth shook her head. "You'll never know the sacrifices I've made for you."

"I have to go. The registration for the reunion is tonight."

"That's what Eden told me. Why on earth would the committee have registration on a Thursday night?"

"I have no idea. But I ought to go and sign up."

"Will you be back for dinner? We're having veal cutlets."

"Not tonight, thanks." He stood and walked to the door. Ruth followed him. "I'll see you tomorrow or the next day."

"Your father saw his mother every day of his life up until the time she died," Ruth pointed out.

"I guess I'm not the son my father was," Trey said with no misgivings. He always felt closed in in his mother's house, and it had nothing to do with the expensive antique furnishings. No matter what he did, it was never quite good enough to please her.

Ruth watched her son leave and walk down the sidewalk to where he had left his car. In many ways he was exactly as she—and his father, of course—had modeled him to be. He was tall, handsome, well-educated, personable. He had married the woman she had hoped he would, and even though they were divorced, Ruth wasn't convinced that they would stay that way. Andrew had told her that a man needed and wanted a son to carry on after him, and Trey surely couldn't be that much different from his father. Someday he would want a son, Andrew McCullough IV, to follow in his footsteps.

She closed the door and went back into the living room. The silence was broken only by the soft ticking of the porcelain clock on the mantel. Ruth liked a silent house. It was a sign of good breeding, according to her mother's teachings. The house where Ruth had grown up was as silent and as well-ordered as this one.

Pouring herself another cup of coffee, she sat back in the white silk chair and reflected on her son's life. Trey was a successful attorney, and Clearwater was a large enough town to give him a profitable practice as it had his father and grandfather before him. All the McCullough men were lawyers. Nothing else had ever been considered for Trey.

His life could have been so different. It could have been ruined before it had started, really. Ruth thought back to Trey's high-school days and how he had rebelled by dating that Branson girl. Ruth actually shuddered when she thought about it. The girl's father, Amos Branson, was the town drunk and her mother cleaned other women's houses. For Ruth, who had never seen her mother or grandmother or any of her husband's female relatives lift a finger to do their own cleaning, this was a stigma beyond comprehension.

The Branson girl hadn't been unattractive, but then some girls of her type did have a sort of low beauty. In her youth, Ruth had known several girls who would have been pretty if they had been able to afford the proper clothes, make-up, and hair styles. But certainly one didn't marry girls like that, and no McCullough should date one. She and Andrew had been horrified when they learned who was wearing Trey's letter jacket. The young couple had been going steady before Ruth had realized the danger of it.

Naturally, Andrew had told her to take care of it, and she had. Ruth was still proud of how effectively she had handled the problem. The McCullough fortune could buy so much. At first Ruth had been skeptical that the girl would keep her part of the bargain, but after a year or so had passed and Hannah hadn't come back to Clearwater, Ruth had breathed a sigh of relief and put her out of her mind. By then, of course, Trey was safely married to Eden and was therefore out of Hannah's grasp anyway.

Ruth frowned as she wondered what had become of Hannah and whether she planned to come back to the class reunion. Surely, Ruth thought, after fifteen years she had nothing to worry about, even if Hannah did return.

By now she must be married and a far cry from the pretty girl Trey had once thought he loved. There was surely no reason to worry.

As Hannah stepped into the high-school cafeteria and looked around for a familiar face, she had the sensation of having stepped into a time warp. How could these adults, all of them hurrying toward middle age, possibly be the boys and girls she had known in school?

She threaded her way through the crowd and signed up at the registration table. That so many were here on a Thursday was startling. She hadn't expected many to be able to get back to town on a weekday. But then, not everyone had moved away, and of those who had, many might still be within driving distance. Clearwater was situated at the edge of the East Texas oil field, and there were numerous towns of various sizes throughout the area.

"Hannah?" a voice asked doubtfully.

Hannah turned to see a woman with curly brown hair and a friendly face. "Kit? It is really you?"

Kit hugged her then stepped back with a grin. "We grew up."

Hannah laughed and felt ridiculously like crying. "I guess we did. We became adults after all, even though we swore we never would."

"I married Mike Holt. Do you remember him?"

"Mike? Wasn't he in the band? I remember."

203

"We have two boys now. Mike is a mechanic and we live in Houston."

"Do you really? I never thought you'd like a city."

"You can get used to anything, I guess. It's convenient for shopping. What about you?"

"I'm in Austin at St. Thomas Hospital."

"A hospital? What are you, a nurse?"

Hannah shook her head. "I'm a doctor."

Kit stared at her. "A doctor? You're kidding!"

"No, I really am. I'm a general practitioner, not a specialist."

"Well, you always did make good grades. I thought you'd be valedictorian."

Hannah smiled and didn't remind Kit that she had been salutatorian. "Is Mike here?"

"He's coming after work tomorrow. We'll leave the boys with my parents. Mike's folks have retired and moved away to be near one of his aunts. Maybe you and I will have time to get to know each other again." She hesitated. "If you want to."

"Of course I do. How do you suppose we ever lost touch in the first place?" Hannah asked, but she knew the answer. At the time she left Clearwater, she wanted to leave as many memories behind as possible. Kit had signed up for a business course at the junior college in Kilgore, and they had developed divergent interests. Hannah hadn't wanted anyone to ask how she had been able to leave town, and she hadn't encouraged correspondence with any of her friends.

"I guess you got a great scholarship," Kit was saying. "We all assumed you must have. I guess you being a doctor proves it. I just can't get over it. A doctor! I had trouble in chemistry class even memorizing the periodic table!"

The crowd parted and Hannah found herself face to face with Eden. There was no way she could pretend not to see her or to recognize her, so Hannah smiled and said hello.

"Why, Hannah Branson, as I live and breathe." Eden came closer and looked Hannah over carefully. "I would never have recognized you."

"No? I'd have known you anywhere."

Kit said quickly, "Hannah was just telling me that she's a doctor now. In Austin."

"Really." Eden's expression showed no interest, and her tone discouraged elaboration. "Who did you marry, Hannah? I can't seem to remember."

Hannah took a deep breath and said calmly, "I didn't marry. I've been busy." She smiled as if such an all-inclusive statement was perfectly reasonable.

Eden smiled and her eyes narrowed. "Kit, have you seen Trey?"

"No, is he here?" Kit glanced at Hannah as if to see how she was handling this.

Hannah didn't comment. She had hoped she would have some time to prepare herself before seeing Trey and that Eden wouldn't still be as beautiful as she had been in school. Except for Eden's more sophisticated hair style and faint wrinkles at the corners of her eyes and mouth, she looked the same as ever.

"Will you excuse me? I have to go find him." Eden nodded a farewell to Kit and turned and walked away.

Hannah remembered to breathe. "I guess they're still married."

"He just married her on the rebound," Kit said loyally. "We all knew it."

"It doesn't matter anymore." Hannah managed a shaky laugh. "That was fifteen years ago, after all."

A man bumped into Hannah and she glanced around to see Trey himself standing at her shoulder. From the expression in his eyes, he was as startled to see her as she was to see him. Hannah's mouth parted and she felt her hands grow cold. The shyness she had overcome made her once more unable to speak.

"Hannah," he said as if to convince himself it was really she.

"Hello, Trey."

Kit eased away. "I'll see you two later."

Hannah opened her mouth to tell Kit to stay, but she had melded into the crowd already. Hannah looked up into Trey's hazel eyes. If it was possible, he had grown more handsome through the years, and he wore confidence like a mantle. She had always thought the Greek gods were no match for Trey McCullough. "Your . . . Eden was looking for you."

"She was? What did she want?"

"How should I know?" Hannah said more tersely than she had planned. "She went toward the soft drink machines." With a Herculean effort, Hannah said, "She's still beautiful."

"Not to me. We're divorced."

The relief that flooded through Hannah made her gasp. "You are? She implied . . ."

"I'm not sure she accepts it, but we are. She's had two husbands since, one from Dallas and one from Chicago, and now she's back to her maiden name again. She always takes back her maiden name. Maybe that way she can pretend those lousy marriages never happened."

Hannah could listen to his voice forever. It was soft and musical and deep. Just hearing him speak excited her. She blinked and reminded herself she couldn't care for him. "I assume you became a lawyer as you'd planned?"

"Yes. What about you? Are you married?"

"No. I live in Austin. I'm a doctor at St. Thomas Hospital."

"A doctor?"

"Surprised? Eden seemed to think I would never amount to much of anything. But maybe I'm giving her too much credit. She might not have been thinking at all." Hannah smiled to ease the barb in her words. She had never liked Eden and knowing Eden had married Trey had done nothing to endear the woman to Hannah.

Trey grinned. "You always did have a way with words. Maybe you should have become a lawyer."

"I'm sorry. I shouldn't have said that about Eden. It's just that she always has been able to irritate me more than anyone else I've ever known."

"I know what you mean." Trey gazed down at her. "You didn't marry."

"No." She gave him no reason. Let him think what he pleased.

"That surprises me more than hearing you're a doctor, frankly. Are the men in Austin blind or just confirmed bachelors?"

"I haven't had much time for socializing. It's not easy to build up a practice and I've had to work long hours to get established." She added, "Not every woman wants to marry."

"I know, but I wouldn't have thought that described you."

Hannah frowned up at him. "I don't recall being particularly dependent. Is that how you saw me?"

"No, I just saw you as having a lot to give in a relationship. I was probably wrong." He continued to smile but now it seemed cooler. "After all, you dropped me rather suddenly, as I recall. No, I wouldn't classify you as dependent."

Hannah drew back. She had forgotten that Trey had no idea why she had broken up with him or why she had refused to write or talk to him after that terrible day. She had been so involved with her own broken heart and her unexpected chance to break free of Clearwater, Texas, and to make something of herself that she had overlooked that Trey must have had a broken heart of his own. She had thought he had accepted the end of their relationship since he had married Eden so quickly. Now she wasn't so sure.

"If you'll excuse me," Trey said. With a slight inclination of his head, he walked away.

Hannah threaded her way back through the crowd and out the door. She had had all the memories she could stand for one day.

Chapter Two

Friday

To take advantage of the unusually warm weather, the reunion committee had decided to have the barbecue outdoors in the park, rather than in the armory building where it was originally planned. Hannah and Kit found each other in the serving line.

"Isn't this weather great?" Kit asked as she put potato salad on her plate. "Whoever would have guessed it would be warm enough to eat outside?"

"It couldn't be better. Who planned this reunion anyway? My letter was signed by Jimmy Isaacs, but I haven't seen him here."

"I suppose he signed the letters because he was class president. No, I heard it was planned by Eden and the other cheerleaders."

"The same ones who did all the party planning

in high school. I would have thought they'd be tired of planning parties by now."

"I've kept up with news of Clearwater, and Eden hasn't changed all that much. She still seems to be more interested in planning parties and shopping than in anything else."

Hannah looked across to where Eden and three other women were engaged in conversation. "She still looks better than anyone has a right to."

"I know. She hasn't gained a pound." Kit sighed and pulled at the bottom of her sweater. She had gained more than a mere pound and had always been sensitive about her weight.

"Trey told me last night that he and Eden are divorced."

"Oh?" Kit looked at Hannah with interest. "You're both single and together for the weekend."

Hannah laughed. "Alone with about a hundred other people."

"That's all right. Magic can still happen. And this *is* Valentine's weekend."

"You always were an incurable romantic."

"I for one am glad there's no vaccination for that. As I recall, you used to believe in romance, too."

"That seems so long ago."

They left the line and headed for the picnic tables. Kit said, "You never did tell me why you and Trey broke up. Do you still remember?"

"It's not something I'm ever likely to forget. But

that's all so far in the past. Tell me about your sons."

As Hannah listened to Kit's enthusiastic re-counting of her sons' most recent activities, she ate and glanced now and then around the crowd looking for Trey. However, he was nowhere to be seen, and she wished that didn't disappoint her.

"Mike will be here before the evening is out," Kit was finishing up. "He's coming as soon as he gets off work." She consulted her watch. "I expect him in an hour or so. I can't wait for you to see him again. Remember how skinny he used to be in school? It's all turned to muscle now."

Hannah made the appropriate responses but she was thinking how Trey had changed, too, and all for the better. He hadn't been nearly as sexy in high school. His smile then had been boyish; now it held a mysterious quality as if he had suffered from some secret pain. She shook her head. That was nonsense. Wasn't it?

When Kit finished her meal, they took the paper plates to the trash cans and wandered over to the swings. "We used to come here every Saturday," Hannah said. "Remember?"

"I sure do. This was where Mike proposed to me."

"He did? At the swings?"

"We were in the second grade at the time. After we graduated, he asked me out and reminded me that I'd said, years before, I would marry him.

You know me—I never go back on a promise."
Kit laughed.

"I guess I'm the same way." Hannah recalled the last time she had seen Trey's mother, Ruth. At the time, the woman had worn her hair curled and it had started graying. What did she look like now? His father had been in poor health, especially for a man in his early forties. She wondered if he was still alive. With her present medical knowledge, she knew Andrew McCullough had been a man waiting for a heart attack. "Do you think there's a statute of limitations on promises?"

"What do you mean?"

"Nothing. I was just talking."

She felt a tingle run up her back, as if someone was watching her. When she turned around, there he was. Their eyes met and for a moment neither moved, then Trey came toward them. Hannah couldn't have turned away. Even with space between them, Trey drew her like a lodestone. She could hear Kit talking, but she was no longer listening.

"Hello." Trey stopped a few feet away as if he wasn't sure of his welcome.

"Hello. I was beginning to think you weren't going to come tonight."

"I was held up at the office."

Kit looked from one to the other. Her eyes were bright with interest. "Well, I guess I'll go over there and see what Mary Jane Morris has been up to the last fifteen years."

Neither Hannah nor Trey heard her.

"Then I think I'll go play in the traffic and maybe fly to the moon."

"What?" Hannah asked, feeling guilty that she hadn't been listening to her friend.

Kit grinned. "I said I'm going to wander around and talk to people. See you two later."

Trey said good-bye, but his eyes never left Hannah. When the two of them were relatively alone, he said, "You really haven't changed all that much. I thought maybe it was a trick of the lights last night."

"Not changed? I'd say I've changed more than anyone else here. Maybe your memory isn't accurate."

"I never saw you that way."

Hannah knew what he meant. In Clearwater it was generally accepted that any relation of Amos Branson had a stigma from birth. Her uncles and cousins had all been in trouble in one way or another, and her father was known by everyone as a mean drunk. "You might have if I'd stayed."

He was quiet for a minute. "Is that why you left me? I know it wasn't for the reasons you said. It couldn't have been, not with what we had between us."

"I was a child. Just eighteen."

"You were more mature than most eighteen-year-olds."

"I had to be. That doesn't mean that I was good at making life-altering decisions."

215

Trey moved closer, and Hannah turned and fell into step with him as if it had been his intention for them to walk away from the others standing close by. She couldn't stay so near that crowd of people. She knew several of them already were speculating on her speaking to Trey at all.

"You never married." He said it as if it was a puzzle he was trying to solve.

"As I told you last night, I've been busy."

He didn't dispute her words, but she could feel his disbelief. That was something they had always had between them, a sort of overdeveloped empathy. They had once teased each other that if one of them bumped a shin, the other would bruise.

They walked down to the edge of the lake. Across the silvery water, Hannah could see the piers and the restaurant that jutted out over the water, the place where all the proms were held and where the reunion dance would take place the following night. Trey narrowed his eyes against the lowering sun and gazed at the pier. "That was where I asked you to go steady."

"It was also where we broke up." She stared at the building. It looked so innocent to have been such a significant part in the shattering of her life. No, she reminded herself, not shattered— rescued. "It's odd how sometimes a thing can be both bad and good, isn't it? It was painful leaving Clearwater and . . . everybody, but if I hadn't, I wouldn't have become a doctor. I might have fulfilled everyone's predictions and never have amounted to anything at all."

"Yes, you would have. It's not in you to fail."

She looked at him. "You don't know that. You don't know anything about me anymore."

"Yes, I do. I may not know the incidents of the past fifteen years, but I've always known who you are." His voice was caressing but touched with pain. "Why did you come back, Hannah?"

She turned her face away. "For the class reunion, of course."

"Nothing else? You didn't make the five- or ten-year reunions. I know because I was here looking for you."

"I was busy."

"I tried to find out where you had gone, but your mother wouldn't tell me."

Hannah glanced up at him in surprise. "You talked to Mama?"

"I wanted to see if you were all right. I didn't know where you were."

"There was no reason for you to know. You were married before I left town." She couldn't keep the recrimination out of her voice.

"You said you never wanted to see me or to speak to me again. At the time I believed it. Now I realize you might have changed your mind if I had been more persistent."

"No, I couldn't. I wouldn't have."

"Why?" He waited for her answer.

Hannah was tempted to tell him the truth, that his mother had called Hannah to come to see her and had offered to pay her way through college on the condition she never see Trey again, and that she had by chance called on a day when Hannah's father was drunker than usual and in a raging tantrum that had sent Hannah running from the house. Ruth had told her that whether or not she accepted the offer, Trey would still break up with her. This, coupled with Hannah's determination to get away somehow from her abusive father, convinced her to agree to Ruth's terms.

She looked into Trey's eyes and knew she couldn't tell him. She had given her word. "We weren't meant to be together. It would have been like harnessing a mule and a thoroughbred to the same wagon. None of your friends would have accepted me."

"Yes, they would have. Most of them already had, if you recall."

"A few, but not the ones who counted."

"That's no reason for you to have done what you did. All my real friends would have come around in time."

"If I had stayed, I would never have become a doctor. You can't dispute that."

"No, but we could have gone to college together."

"At the time I didn't think so. Besides, you already must have been interested in Eden for you to have married her so quickly."

"Eden marries everyone quickly."

She smiled and picked up a pebble and threw

it into the water. How could a long-ago hurt be so raw and tender now?

"Have you been back in town since that summer?"

"A few times. Not often. You know how Papa is. It's better if I keep my distance."

"How is your mother?"

"Tired. She's worn out with work and looks ten years older than she really is. I tried to convince her to come back to Austin with me, but she won't leave Clearwater."

"Not long ago I considered leaving, too, but changed my mind."

"Your mother wouldn't have liked that." She bit back the words. As far as Trey knew, Hannah had never met Ruth.

"About two years ago my father died. He had been in bad health for quite some time, but he died of a sudden, massive heart attack, and Mother needed me to help her get over the shock. That was one of the reasons I decided not to move away. Then I had not only my own law practice to think about but his as well. It would have been a shame to leave it all behind and have to start over."

"I know. I've felt trapped by circumstances, too."

"Kit is looking good," he said as a silence grew between them.

"She's happy. She talks about Mike all the time."

"She married Mike Holt, didn't she?"

"Yes. I didn't know if you remembered him."

"I tried to find her after my divorce to see if she had your new address at college, but I couldn't locate her."

"She and Mike live in Houston."

"I never thought to try there. Most of the ones in our class who left town ended up in Dallas or Fort Worth. Quite a few never left at all."

"What do you suppose it is about Clearwater that makes people want to stay here or to come back if they've moved away?"

"I don't know. Do you want to come back?"

She hesitated because she wanted to do just that, but couldn't. "Not really. I mean, Clearwater already has several doctors, and I do like to eat and pay my bills. I have a thriving practice in Austin."

"Of our four doctors, two are old enough to retire and one is considering leaving town. He's not from here and hasn't fallen under the Clearwater spell." Trey studied her face. "It never occurred to me that you might come back."

"I'm not coming back," she said rather tersely. "I have no intention of returning to Clearwater. I don't even come back to visit my folks very often."

"So you've been here a number of times in the past fifteen years and I never knew it?"

"I didn't know I was supposed to send a bulletin to the McCullough clan to announce my arrivals and departures."

"Why are you losing your temper?"

"I'm not!" She pushed her hair back from her face in exasperation. Trey always could see right into her mind. "I love Austin, and I wouldn't leave there for my weight in gold."

Trey nodded, and a muscle tightened in his jaw. "Good. I can see we would never get along."

"You can't see anything of the kind. Besides, we wouldn't have to be friends, just because I moved back."

"That's right. You could keep to your medical practice and I could keep to my legal one. There would be no reason for our paths to cross."

"Right." She folded her arms across her chest and wondered how they had managed to get into an argument after so little time together. Then she remembered their love had never gone smoothly. "I had assumed age had mellowed you. But I was wrong. You would still argue with a fence post, if it would argue back."

"And you're still as infuriating as ever. It's no wonder we broke up."

"Thanks!" She glared at him. "If you're always this hard to get along with, I can see why Eden left you."

"That's not why she left. Her boyfriend talked her into it." He stopped suddenly as if he had said more than he had intended.

"She was having an affair? While she was married to you?" Hannah couldn't imagine being interested in any other man if she could have Trey.

"Don't spread it around. No one but Mother knows why we split up."

"What do you think I'm going to do with the information? Have it printed in the paper? How long were you married?" She tried not to feel so sorry that Trey's marriage hadn't been happy.

"About two years. That was a year longer than it should have been. We never were what you'd call happy. I tried to make it work, but there wasn't anything to save when it came right down to it. I think Eden wanted to marry me because she wanted to get married and it didn't really matter to whom."

"Or she may have seen you as someone she couldn't get easily." Hannah was remembering how Eden had taunted her about having dated Trey the weekend after they broke up. After fifteen years Hannah still felt the hurt. "She always seemed to want whatever she couldn't have."

"That's Eden, all right." He started strolling along the lake's shore. "Are you seeing anyone in Austin? Seriously, I mean?"

"The world doesn't revolve around romance! No, I'm not dating anyone, and that's the way I want it."

"You're not dating anyone at all?" He glanced down at her in amazement. "Not at all?"

"I meant not seriously. Of course I date." She didn't want him to know how lonely she was. She risked a sideways look at him. "What about you?"

"No, no one seriously."

"Too bad." She wondered if that meant he was lonely, too.

"It'll be getting dark soon."

"Most likely. It generally does when the sun goes down." The sun was already hanging on the treetops beyond the lake. The water was taking on the hues of pink and blue in the early sunset.

"The park closes at dark unless there's a ball game."

Hannah looked back and saw most of the crowd had already left the picnic grounds. She had lost all track of time.

"Would you like to come to my house and catch up old times?" He waited for her answer.

Hannah wanted to go with him more than she wanted air to breath. "No, I don't think that would be a good idea."

He straightened. "No, I suppose it isn't. You'll be at the brunch tomorrow?"

"Yes. And the dance later."

"I guess I'll see you there then."

He seemed reluctant for them to part, so Hannah turned decisively and started for the parking area. If he asked her to go with him to the dance, she wasn't sure she would be strong enough to refuse. She wished she didn't regret not going home with him. For perhaps the millionth time, she wished she had never made that promise to his mother.

223

*   *   *

Trey watched Hannah walk to her car before going to his. She was infuriating and as stubborn as ever. What was it about her that made him unable even to see another woman as long as she was near? He drove to his mother's house, because he didn't want to be alone at the moment.

"Trey, how nice to see you," Ruth said as he came into the den. "I thought you'd be at the reunion."

"The park was about to close. Whoever canceled the reservation for the armory building didn't take sunset into consideration."

"That would have been Eden, I suppose. She was the one making most of the plans since the other girls all live out of town."

Trey didn't want to talk about Eden tonight. "I saw Hannah Branson."

"Oh? I had assumed she would be there. Why do you mention it?" She waited for an answer.

Trey wondered why she cared. She had never met Hannah and had always been against his dating her. "I asked her to spend some time with me this evening. She turned me down," he added.

Ruth relaxed visibly. "That's just as well. You know how she treated you in high school. Those Bransons are simply no good."

"Hannah's not like the rest of her father's family. She must have taken after her mother."

"Her mother? Oh, you mean Leah Branson. She works Thursdays for Ouida Clark."

Trey didn't miss the implication that the Bransons might be okay as hired help, assuming it wasn't Amos, but not as social contacts. "You're a snob, Mother," he said with no rancor.

"I'm no such thing. What a way to talk to your mother." Although Ruth frowned at her son, she wasn't really upset.

"Hannah is a doctor now. She's a professional just as I am and in a city far bigger than Clearwater. Hannah doesn't fit in the Branson mold."

"Son, you don't know that. After all, she broke up with you for no good reason that you ever told me and you've said she never so much as wrote to you in all these years."

Trey nodded. That was a fact. "Why do you suppose she did that? I guess she thought I was still married to Eden."

"She must have heard about your divorce. Everyone in Clearwater knows everyone else's business."

"Not necessarily. I couldn't tell you a single thing about her family."

"My point exactly. Our families don't have any reason to know each other. I'm glad she was sensible enough to turn you down tonight."

Trey wasn't convinced. "You don't know her, Mother. Hannah isn't at all the way you assume she is."

Ruth looked concerned for a moment, then wiped the anxiety from her face with a smile.

"Well, that's neither here nor there. She will be gone after Sunday, and you probably will never see her again."

The prospect wasn't pleasing to Trey. Hannah might be infuriating, but he couldn't bear the idea of not seeing her again; it had taken him too long to find her. "I ought to be going. See you later."

Ruth stood to protest, but Trey stopped her words with a smile. "Whatever you say, son. Come for dinner Sunday."

"If I can't, I'll call and let you know."

"That's fine. I'm sure you and the other football players have a lot of catching up to do this weekend."

Trey didn't tell her he had no interest in his former teammates except for the few he had kept in contact with. There was no reason to let her know it was a woman he wanted to spend time with. He decided to call Hannah as soon as he got home.

Hannah sat with her mother at the kitchen table. So much of their time together had been spent over this old table with its chrome legs and gray-flecked Formica top. Leah wrapped her large knuckled hands around the coffee mug and crossed her legs. "Was there a good many people at the park?"

"More than at the registration yesterday. I think some weren't able to get in until this evening."

Leah nodded. "Folks have to work. That's a fact."

"Mama, please think about coming back to Austin with me." Hannah leaned forward and covered her mother's hands with her own. "Even if it's only for a visit."

"I can't do that. Who would look after your daddy?"

"He's a grown man. He can look after himself."

Leah shook her head and lifted the cup to her lips. "If I was not to show up at my job, I'd be fired. Then where would we be? No, I can't go to Austin."

"I can support you. I make a lot of money."

"Would you support your daddy, too?" Leah asked astutely.

Hannah drew back. "I would if he'd stop drinking."

"I don't reckon he can stop. It's been going on so long now it's a part of him. Like breathing."

Hannah knew there was no point in arguing. Years before she had tried to explain to her mother that he could get help through AA and her through Al–anon, but her mother hadn't listened. It would be pointless to try to get her to understand the concepts of co-dependency and to recognize herself as an enabler. "I worry about you."

"No need to do that. I'm healthy and I still have a good many years in me yet. I'll let you know when to start worrying." She stood and stretched. "I think I'm going to go on to bed. Your daddy will be in shortly, but there's no need to wait up for him."

Hannah nodded. "I think I'll sit up and read for a while."

When Leah was gone, Hannah rinsed the two cups and the coffee pot. Leaving them to drain in the rack, she went into the living room. There were almost no books in the house. Neither of her parents were much on reading and there had been no extra money for Leah to buy many books. She picked up a worn copy of *Gone With the Wind* and opened it at random. As she had thought it would, it fell open at the place where Rhett convinced Scarlett to marry him. Between the pages lay a dried flower.

Hannah sat on the lumpy couch and touched the flower gently. A pale blue petal detached and fell into the margin of the book. She remembered the day Trey had given it to her. They had been out on the pier at the lake and he had asked her to go steady with him. When they left the pier, he had seen the wildflower and picked it for her. Hannah had pressed it into her favorite passage of her favorite book.

She closed the book and ran her hand over the book's faded dust jacket. She could remember poring over the book and wishing that someday she would be able to get out from under the poverty and social stigma of being Amos Branson's child. Her only escape as a child had been in books, and she had treasured the few she owned.

Again she opened the book to the flower. When she had put it there, she had thought her world was perfect. Trey McCullough, the cutest boy in school and captain of the football team, wanted to go steady with her and in only a few short months she would graduate from high school, the first girl in her family ever to do so. It had seemed as if her life had been blessed by a fairy godmother.

She had loved Trey from the very beginning and he had loved her, too. That was why Ruth McCullough felt it necessary to go to the trouble and expense of getting rid of her. Ruth had known her son well enough to realize he wouldn't give up Hannah for any reason. But Hannah had had an Achilles's heel.

Hannah heard a car pull up and two doors slam. She automatically glanced up as the front door opened. It was her father and his favorite drinking buddy, his cousin, Jud. Both were obviously drunk. Hannah stood up and started from the room.

"Wait a minute. Hold on," Amos said to his daughter. "Ain't you got nothing to say to your own cousin?" He steadied himself against the doorframe.

"Hello, Jud." She didn't smile.

"Hey, Hannah. You sure changed a lot since you was just a skinny little kid with red hair and freckles. Ain't she, Amos? Whoever woulda thought a youngun of yours would be so pretty?"

Amos grinned and rocked back on his heels unsteadily. "She looks a bit like Leah did at that age, don't she?"

Hannah couldn't imagine her mother ever not looking tired to the bone and old. She turned to go to her room.

"Now don't go rushing off," Amos said as he weaved over to her and put out his hand to catch her arm but missed. "Sing us that song like I taught you."

"I don't have any idea what you're talking about. Good night."

"You know the one. The song about the preacher that went a-courting."

"It's late and I've long since forgotten the song. I'm going to bed."

"I remember it," Jud exclaimed as he threw back his head and bellowed out the song with no regard to the tune.

"Hush! You'll wake the neighbors!" Hannah frowned at the men. "Jud, you be quiet or you have to go home."

Amos drew himself up. "No daughter of mine is going to be so sassy to her elders. Jud is a guest in this house."

"Jud is drunk and so are you. Keep your voices down." Hannah had always been afraid of her father when he was drunk. She hadn't always been sure he wouldn't hurt her or mistakenly leave the gas jets on or the doors unlocked all night. Amos wasn't to be trusted when he was this far into a bottle. "Jud, I think you'd better go home."

Jud looked as if he were about to pout. He wasn't a mean drunk, just a maudlin one.

Amos lifted his arm and took a swing at Hannah. His movements were so slow she had no trouble ducking. "That does it!" she fumed as she pushed her father toward his bedroom door. "Jud, get out of here!"

Amos kept up a stream of complaints, but she pushed Jud out the door and locked it. She heard his unsteady footsteps going across the porch and down the steps. He didn't have far to go as he only lived two houses down.

Amos lowered his head like a bull about to charge. "You've gone too far, miss. I've a mind to take off my belt!"

Hannah felt sick. In the intervening years she had forgotten what it was like to live under the same roof with her father. Keeping her voice level and her face expressionless, she said, "If you touch me, I'll call the police." The threat was strong enough to stall him until she could go into her bedroom and shut the door.

She had no more than pushed the bolt into place securing the door when Amos began hammering on the door with his fists. She sat on the bed and hugged her book to her. Large tears filled her eyes and ran down her cheeks. She heard her mother's voice soothing and cajoling Amos into calming down and going to bed. In a few moments she heard the door of their bedroom click shut. Hannah lay back and looked up at the water stains on the bedroom ceiling. At times like this, she knew why she had been so easily persuaded to leave Trey and to get out of Clearwater. It might have been her only chance. But it had been a terrible price to pay. Hannah allowed herself to cry.

Chapter Three

Saturday Morning

"I feel out of place here," Kit murmured to Hannah. "It's so expensive! Of course they've given us a group rate, but still!"

"I know. I feel uneasy here, too." Hannah wasn't awed by the Pier House restaurant's high costs, for she was accustomed to going to far more expensive places than this in Austin, but Pier House had employed her father—when he was sober enough to work—and she couldn't forget that.

"Let's play miniature golf," Mike suggested. "I haven't played in years."

They strolled over the manicured lawn to the miniature golf club rental booth. Kit chose a putter and swung it experimentally. "Remember when we were in the ninth grade and our school trip was to Longview to play miniature golf?"

"How could I forget," Hannah said with a laugh.

233

"The first ball you hit went sailing across the way and hit the teacher."

"I had never played before," Kit protested. "I had only seen golf on TV and they always hit the ball hard."

Mike laughed. "I have a feeling I'm going to win this game."

"Don't be too sure," Hannah countered. "You know what they say about doctors always being on the golf course. I may not have played in a long time, but surely I soaked up some expertise from the doctors I work with."

"I'll take my chances," Mike said.

Kit put her fluorescent green ball on the tee-off mat. "Let's stay in touch, Hannah. I've missed you."

"I've missed you, too. I'm not much for writing letters, but I'm great with a long-distance calling card."

Kit's ball veered to the right, missing the cup by quite a distance, and bounced off the back board. Hannah put hers in place. "I can do better than that."

When hers slewed to the left and lodged itself behind the deflector board, Mike laughed and sent his within inches of the hole. "Just luck," Kit commented. "We're letting you build your confidence so we can smash you later."

Hannah enjoyed being with Kit and Mike and not having to think about work for a change. She hadn't noticed before, but she hadn't forgotten about work in months, maybe in years.

"Your turn," Kit said. "What were you thinking about?"

"I was trying to remember how long it's been since I had a vacation. A real one, not just a trip to some medical conference." Her second putt fell a bit short, and she tapped it in so her ball wouldn't be in the way.

"You should see a doctor," Mike teased. "All work and no play isn't healthy." Mike sank his ball with relative ease.

"You're a fine one to talk," his wife chided. "Mike goes to the station early and stays late nearly every day." Kit managed to get her ball down on the fifth stroke.

"I have a responsibility to Houston," he said in mock seriousness. "I have to keep all those cars rolling or we may run low on exhaust pollution."

"It's good to be back in the country where you can't see the air," Kit admitted.

"And at night you *can* see the stars."

As play continued, Hannah found herself having so much fun, she hated to see the last hole coming.

Poising herself carefully over her ball, Hannah stroked the ball like a pro, sending it straight down the green alley toward the ninth hole. "Ha! A hole in one!"

"I demand a recount," Mike protested.

At the last hole Hannah and Mike were tied, but

this shot sent her ahead by one point. "I won!" she cried as excited as a teenager. "I have you by one point!"

"And you're such a gracious and humble winner, too," Mike jested with a phony grimace. "Let's play again."

Hannah looked up to see Trey coming toward them. "Maybe later."

Kit followed her look. "It's Trey. I guess that shows you how we rate. Come on, Mike, I'll play you again. I think I have the hang of it now."

Hannah met Trey halfway. His hair, touched with sunlight, gleamed like gold, and she thought that he looked more than ever like a Greek god. "I see you don't work on Saturday."

He shook his head. "Not usually. I'm afraid I don't fit the standard of a professional automatically being a workaholic."

"I'm afraid I do. I was just telling Kit and Mike that I can't remember the last time I had a vacation."

They fell into step easily and skirted the miniature golf course. Some of the alumni had brought their offspring to the park with them, and the shouts and shrieks of playing children mingled with the adult conversation. Some of the men were organizing a softball game in the green area past the concession stand.

"I'm surprised you're not playing ball," she said. "I see Jimmy Isaacs over there."

"I can play softball with Jimmy Isaacs any time.

I can't see you but once every fifteen years."

"Oh? You intend to see me again in the year 2008?"

"That makes it sound like a millennium away."

"We'll only be forty-eight. The time after that, we'll be sixty-three. And the time after that—"

"Never mind. I get the point." He grinned down at her. "We could compress that a bit and agree to see each other before then."

"Do you come to Austin often?"

"No."

"Too bad. I seldom come to Clearwater. I guess I'll see you in 2008, assuming I'm able to come that weekend."

"I could come to Austin. Just because my work doesn't take me there very often doesn't mean I can't come anyway. There is more to life than work, you know."

"Is there? Sometimes I forget."

"What would you tell one of your patients who said such a thing?"

"I'm not one of my patients, and I know better than to admit how much I work to another doctor."

"I know what you need. You need a ride on the merry-go-round."

"The what?" She laughed and looked to the painted horses on the carousel. "I haven't been on a merry-go-round since I was a child."

"Just as I thought." He bought two tickets, and they found horses side by side.

Hannah slid her leg over the wooden saddle and was surprised at how young it made her feel. The music started and the horses lurched forward. As they picked up speed and began the loping motion, she laughed and looked over at Trey. "This is fun!"

"See? I told you it's what you needed. I think you should make a concentrated effort to ride a merry-go-round at least once a month."

"Are you saying you come here that often?"

"No way. I have my professional standing in the community to protect." He laughed as if nothing could be farther from the truth.

Hannah was sorry when the ride ended. She had enjoyed the brief trip back to childhood. They left the carousel, and Hannah pointed to the concession stand. "Snow cones!"

She bought them each a blue one, and they walked as they ate.

"My nose is freezing," Trey commented. "February is no time for snow cones."

"Nonsense. Your nose will turn blue before it freezes. I'll keep an eye on it." She was glad she had worn a sweatshirt instead of the blouse she had first picked out, because the air had turned nippy overnight. "I hope the nice weather holds until after tonight."

"It probably will. Even if it doesn't, the dance is indoors. How about going with me?"

"No."

"That's plain enough."

"I meant that I would prefer having my own car there. Call it a holdover from my being on call so often. But I'll meet you there."

"You still don't want me coming to your parents' house?"

"You haven't forgotten that?"

"I remember everything about you."

Hannah told herself not to let his statement mean too much. She still couldn't have him. "Papa still drinks. The neighborhood has gone down hill."

"I know. I live here. Remember?"

"I didn't know you ever had reason to go on that side of town."

"I don't, but I pass near there from time to time. Clearwater is a small town. I don't think it's a good idea for you to go there alone after dark."

"That's silly. My parents live there. I lived there myself for eighteen years." She paused. "Is it really that bad?"

"It is. This is between the two of us, but there's reason to think some drug dealers may be on that street and not far from where your parents live."

"I've tried to convince Mama to move away. I want her to come to Austin, but you'd think it was on the moon to hear her talk."

"At any rate, I want to pick you up and take you home."

"I guess it couldn't hurt," she said slowly. She wished her heart wasn't racing at the prospect of a date with Trey. "But it's only because of the neighborhood."

"Why are so determined to keep me at arm's length?"

"Why do you say that?"

"You know what I mean. Neither of us is married, so what difference would it make if we date? Surely whatever happened fifteen years ago between us can't still be that important. I don't even remember why we broke up."

"I do." She shook her head. "I can't talk about it, Trey. Just take my word for it. We shouldn't make more out of this weekend than it is."

"You haven't been watching a rerun of *Summer Place* on TV, have you? We're adults, and we can see each other if we want to. I know how to get to Austin if you won't come here. We could pick up where we left off."

"We can't get along for two hours running! Don't you remember last night? We had barely begun to talk before we were arguing."

"That wasn't an argument, it was a heated discussion. So what? We aren't arguing now, are we?"

"Would you believe me if I said I really do have a man in Austin whom I'm serious about?"

"No, I wouldn't. If you did, you'd have told me yesterday when I asked you and you wouldn't have agreed to go out with me tonight."

"Maybe I've changed. Maybe I'm not as trustworthy as I used to be. Maybe I'm cheating behind his back. Did you think of that?"

"I think you're the most unaccomplished liar I've ever met, and if I had you on the witness stand, I would be able to tear holes in that story. You don't have someone else. Tell me the real truth. Why don't you want to see me?"

She sighed. He was right. She had never been good at lying. "I can't discuss it. I really can't."

He was silent for a while. "Hannah, you don't have something wrong with you, do you? I mean like some disease that you don't want to tell me about?"

"No," she said quickly. "No, that's not it at all. Really, Trey, you're making more of this than it deserves."

"You're a confusing lady," he said. "You always did keep me off balance."

"Eat your snow cone," she advised, "and don't worry so much. I'm here now and we're together. Let tomorrow take care of itself." She wished she could follow her own advice.

When it was time for the brunch to be served, she and Trey went into the Pier House and found seats with Kit and Mike. The fare consisted of a croissant, a sliver of ham, and a bit of fruit.

"This is all?" Trey whispered. "Eden must have chosen the menu."

Mike laughed. "We can go out for burgers when this is over."

As Trey had suspected, Eden was responsible for the menu, and she wasn't reluctant to take credit for it when Jimmy Isaacs stood up to say so. Eden took the floor to a spattering of applause and said, "The brunch is sponsored by the other cheerleaders as well as myself. Stand up, girls, and let everyone see where you are."

Four other women, not all of them still as slim and young-looking as Eden, stood up and received applause. They sat down, and Eden gave them each a benevolent smile. "I want to remind everyone of the dance tonight. It will be right here at Pier House and will start promptly at eight. However, since I know all of us want to be together as much as possible, I've arranged for the pier to be open for drinks earlier, if you care to come."

"She's all heart," Mike mumbled.

Kit poked him and gave him a wifely warning glance.

"Oh, that's right. I forgot you used to be married to Eden," he said to Trey.

"It's okay. It was a long time ago." Trey looked at Hannah, but she was pretending to be engrossed with her croissant.

Eden mentioned the names of several of their former classmates, who had been responsible for mailing cards, setting up hotel accommodations, and making other arrangements, and sat down.

"You know, I always said I'd never come to a class reunion," Kit said. "Why go see people you never bothered to keep in contact with? Now I'm glad I came. Otherwise, I wouldn't have seen Hannah again. At least not this soon."

"That's true," Mike said. "And you'd have missed out on this terrific meal."

Kit laughed and poked him again. "Mike thinks it's not food unless it's meat and potatoes."

As the waitresses removed the plates, waiters served what appeared to be dessert. "What is this?" Mike asked suspiciously.

"Could be flan," Trey ventured. "I'm not sure." He leaned toward Hannah. "Do you want to get out of here and get that hamburger?"

Hannah smiled and nodded, assuming Kit and Mike would come as well. Then it could hardly be considered a date; it was more like a group gathering. She stood up.

Mike tried to stand up as well, but Kit pulled him back down. "I'm not ready yet," she said smugly. "You two go on and we'll meet you later."

"What are you talking about?" her husband said. "I'm hungry."

Kit waved her fingers at Hannah and Trey. "See you later."

Hannah could hardly sit back down, since Trey was waiting for her to leave with him. She tried not to look dismayed as she followed him out of the restaurant. That they were the center of attention had not escaped her notice.

"Do I get the feeling that Kit is matchmaking?" Trey said as they walked to the parking lot.

"She isn't too subtle about it, is she?"

"I've always liked her."

"Trey, don't start in on me. Let's just enjoy today and not worry about the future."

"I'd love to, but I don't have that option. It's taken me fifteen years to find you again, and I don't want you to disappear for another fifteen. I don't have the luxury of moving at a slower pace."

When they reached his car, he opened the door for her and helped her in. As she watched him walk around to his door, she let herself pretend that it was all as simple as he thought, that she hadn't made that foolish promise so many years ago and that she wasn't so determined always to keep her word.

Trey drove to the local drive-in burger haven and gave their order to the man over the intercom. To Hannah, he said, "I hope you don't mind eating in the car. It's more private here."

"It's not terribly private. This is the busiest place in town."

"We'll pretend the other cars don't exist. We used to do that."

"I remember." She smiled. "We were so young. It's hard to believe we were ever so naive."

"Naive? In what way?"

"Every way." She looked down at her clasped hands in her lap. "It's as though I was a different person then. Or at least it seems that way when I'm in Austin. Then I come back here and it's as if I never really left." She hesitated and added, "Papa was drinking heavily last night. He frightened me."

Trey put his hand over hers. "I wondered if that was what was wrong."

She let him think that was all. "When he gets that way, I don't know what to do. That's the main reason I seldom come back to visit. I don't see why Mama puts up with it day after day. I wouldn't."

"Your mother is from a different generation. I see it in court often. A woman your mother's age and with her level of education often feels she has no choice but to stay married, no matter how bad her life is. She's more afraid of being alone than of living with a man who isn't good to her."

"But it's so unnecessary! Mama is the only one making any money these days. She's not dependent on him for anything."

"That doesn't matter. She probably feels she would be deserting him if she left."

Hannah looked at him. "That's exactly what she said!"

"As I said, I see it all the time. Not just in divorce cases, but in battering ones as well. I'm not saying your father would hurt your mother, but it's the same principle."

"I'm not so sure he wouldn't hurt her."

"Oh?"

"When Papa drinks, he gets mean. These days all he does is drink." She glanced at him. "I shouldn't be telling you all this."

"It's not as if we're strangers, Hannah. I already know your father has a drinking problem."

245

"It's not something I talk about. I'm worried about Mama, though. Trey, you see her. She looks so old and tried. She says she's never sick, but I'm not sure I believe her. It's the sort of thing a mother says to keep someone she loves from worrying about her."

"You could come home more often." He stroked her hand with his thumb. "You could keep a closer eye on them."

"My being around just keeps Papa stirred up. We've never been able to get along. You know what it was like." She smiled sadly. "You're the only person I've ever talked to about my father. Not even Kit knows how bad it was. Not really. But I suppose she guessed. When I was still living at home, I went to her house far more often than we came to mine."

"You could have him hospitalized."

"I know that. But Mama won't hear of it. According to her, his drinking doesn't bother her, and she says to leave it alone. I don't believe her, but what can I do? If I have him committed against both their wishes, they may never speak to me again. They are my parents, after all."

"I know it sounds calloused, but they are adults and have to make their own decisions."

"I realize that, but I can see Mama getting worse every time I visit. You're going to laugh, but I've even considered moving back here."

"You have?" His hazel eyes became alert and his thumb stopped stroking her hand.

"I tried so hard to get out of Clearwater, and now I'm considering coming back. I should have my head examined."

"Not in my opinion. You have a lot to offer to the community. I told you yesterday, we'll be losing two of our doctors soon. I think they would have already retired if it wasn't for the third one wanting to leave town. That would leave us with only one doctor, and Clearwater is too large for one man to carry the entire patient load."

Hannah looked out the window and watched the cars pass by. "I don't want to move back. I'm afraid of getting trapped and not being able to leave again if I find out I can't take it here. I know what people used to say about my being Amos Branson's daughter. I can't be myself here."

"Yes, you can. That was a long time ago. People can see you aren't like him. You worked your way through four years of college and then medical school. It's clear you aren't the same sort of person as your father."

Hannah was quiet for a long while, and Trey wondered if he had said too much. It was a delicate subject. It was one thing for a daughter to say her father was a worthless drunk and quite another for someone else to say it. "Hannah?"

"I'm afraid to move back," she said softly.

Trey tried to weigh his motives. Did he want her back just so he could see her? Was there anything wrong with that? He reached up and brushed her hair back from her face. "You always have had

247

the prettiest hair I've ever seen."

She smiled. "No one has said anything like that to me in a long time. And you shouldn't say it either."

"Why not?" He couldn't understand why she was so determined to keep him at a distance. Couldn't she see he still cared for her?

"Because I can't come back here, not really, and you can't come to Austin. Our worlds don't meet. I don't want to get something started that can't be finished."

"That's not necessarily true." He studied her enchanting dark gray eyes and her luxuriant auburn hair. Just looking at her gave him satisfaction. "If two people want something bad enough, it can usually be accomplished."

"Do you really believe that?" she asked. When her eyes met his, Trey found himself unable to look away.

"Yes. I really believe it. I've seen it happen. You must have seen it, too."

"But what if there is something standing in the way? Something that can't be revealed and can't be ignored?"

"I've learned that communication is our most important skill. If two people can talk and really hear each other, it's amazing what they can work through."

"You make it sound so simple."

"Why do I get the feeling that your leaving me had nothing to do with me at all?" He saw her start and knew he had hit upon a clue. It was a ploy that had worked for him in court countless times. "A feeling that someone else is involved."

A carhop tapping on his window spoiled the moment, and he repressed a groan. Of all times for the hamburgers to arrive. After being interrupted, Hannah likely would retreat back into her shell. Trey rolled down the window, paid for their food, and took the sack from the carhop. "Thanks."

He handed a burger and fries to Hannah, noticing that she showed no interest at all in the food. "Let's go to the park to eat," he suggested. "This is too public."

He drove to the park and stopped his car beside the lake. Hannah still hadn't spoken. "You need someone to talk to," he said. "I'm right here."

She gave him a weak smile. "You're the one person I can't confide in. You'll have to take my word for it."

He sighed. "In that case, let's eat."

They sat at a concrete picnic table not far from the water's edge, and several fat ducks waddled closer in hopes of a handout. As they ate, they gazed at the ducks and water. For a long time, neither of them spoke. Finally Hannah said, "You're the only person I've ever been able to share silence with."

He grinned. "I never heard it put that way."

"It's true. Most people can't abide silence. It makes them nervous. They have to find something to talk about, even if it's mundane or repetitive."

"Silence is as important as words at times. Maybe it's because you and I have always seemed to be on the same wave length. You know we used to say we could read each other's thoughts."

"I know. Those were happy times. At least they were happy when we were together. Then I had to go home." She gazed at the gently rippling water. "I never liked going home."

"It wouldn't be the same if you moved back. You would have your own place. You wouldn't have to go back and confront your father every day."

"I know, but he would come to me. Papa isn't shy about asking me for money." She tossed the ducks a french fry. "I can't give him money because he just spends it on alcohol. I send some to Mama from time to time, but I suspect she just gives it to Papa. I refuse to finance his drinking." She drew in a deep breath. "If I lived here, I would have a better idea what they need. I could take them food or pay the bills and not have to risk giving them money."

"That's true."

Hannah shook her head. "I'm talking nonsense. I can't move back. I have my own life in Austin and I'm happy there. I really am."

"I never said you weren't."

"You were probably thinking it."

He laughed. "No, I wasn't. I was trying to think of a way to coerce you into coming back."

"You're the main reason I can't," she said as she turned to look at him. "I can't seem to get you out of my mind." She turned away. "I shouldn't have said that."

"You don't have to put distance between us. I've never forgotten you, Hannah. I've never stopped caring for you." To his surprise, her eyes brimmed with tears.

Fighting for emotional control, she said, "You have to, Trey. We don't have a future. Not together."

"Why not? Damn it, Hannah, stop talking like a whirligig."

She had to smile. "A whirligig?"

"You know what I mean. You're going in circles. First you say you want to come back, then you say you can't. Then you say you care for me, then you say you don't want to see me. Are you trying to be confusing or am I missing something?"

"I'm confused, too. Have you ever seen what happens to a piece of fish food tossed into a school of minnows? That's the way I feel, pulled at from every side and unable to go forward." She rubbed her eyes. "I should be getting home. Mama doesn't work this afternoon and we're going shopping."

"I'll take you back to your car." He stood and they walked back to his car and paused at the passenger door. "Hannah, I really am here if you want to talk. When we were in high school, I loved you and you loved me. I have no idea what went wrong with us then, but I do know it can be made right again. All you have to do is tell me what's bothering you so we can put it straight again."

"I wish it were that simple, Trey. If it were, I would have been back years ago."

He was thoroughly confused. Without waiting for him to help her, she opened the car door, got in, and shut the door behind her. She wasn't going to elaborate, and he couldn't force a confidence out of her. At least, he thought, he would be with her tonight. He tried not to think that it might be the last time he would ever see her.

Chapter Four

Saturday Night

"Amos, I told you I gave you all the money. Mrs. Isaacs didn't want me to come but for half a day today."

Hannah lifted her head at the sound of her mother's voice. The thin walls of the house did little to muffle sound. Leah and Amos were in the kitchen arguing.

"I don't believe you. Mrs. Isaacs always has you come all day on Saturday." Amos was drunk and belligerent.

"Usually, that's true. This weekend her daughter-in-law was coming over, and they was having some kind of a tea party for some friends. She sent me home at noon."

"You're lying! She can't do that! Don't she know you have an agreement to work every Saturday all day? I'm going to call her up and chew her out!"

Lynda Trent

"Don't you do that! You'll cost me my job."

Hannah closed her eyes and laid her head on her folded arms. How many times had she heard similar arguments? Looking back, it seemed as if her childhood had been a series of arguments between her parents or of tiptoeing around to keep from arousing her father from a drunken sleep. She lifted her head and gazed into her dresser mirror. Dr. Hannah Branson looked back. Everything had changed, yet nothing had changed.

"Amos, if you was to get a job, we wouldn't have to worry so much about folks like Mrs. Isaacs," Leah pointed out to her husband. "You don't have to spend every minute out carousing with Jud and his gang."

"Don't you go to telling me what to do or not to do!" Amos raised his voice in sodden fury. The slurring of his words did little to diminish the evidence of his anger.

Hannah picked up her hair brush and slowly pulled it through her hair. She was trying to decide whether to pretend she was unaware of her parents' argument or go to her mother's aid. Leah seemed to be handling matters, so she stayed put. A glance at her wristwatch told her Trey would be coming to pick her up in twenty minutes.

"Don't you turn your back on me!" Amos bellowed. "You're holding out! I know it!"

"Quit yelling. Do you want Hannah to know we're fighting?"

"I don't care what she knows or don't know. It

ain't as if she ain't never heard us fight before."

Leah's voice sounded tired. "I wish you'd wait until she's gone to throw your fit. We don't get to see her all that often."

"That's because she thinks she's too high and mighty for us. Coming down here when she feels like it and sassing around like the queen of Sheba." He raised his voice so Hannah couldn't miss hearing him. "I wish she'd go on back to Austin where she belongs instead of eating us out of house and home."

Hannah felt sick. Her father had reached the point of drink where he was ready to find fault with everything and everybody. Slowly, she stood and opened her bedroom door. After drawing a deep breath, she went to the phone in the living room and dialed Trey's number. "Hello, Trey? Yes, it's Hannah. Listen, something's come up and I'm going to have to meet you there. No, I'll be there."

She hung up the phone and went to the kitchen. Not waiting for an acknowledgment of her presence, she said, "If you want me to leave, Papa, just say so."

Leah gave him an accusing glare. "He don't want nothing of the sort. Do you, Amos?"

He glared at them both. "What were you doing? Listening to our private talk?"

"I could hardly help it. You know you can hear everything in this house." She turned to Leah. "I'll be leaving early tomorrow morning."

Lynda Trent

"No, baby, stay awhile longer," Leah protested, her eyes begging Hannah not to go. "Don't let this chase you off."

"I'm not, Mama. I have to be at the hospital early Monday morning, and I don't want to be on the road late."

"There she goes," Amos growled. "Throwing it up to us that she's a highfalutin' doctor and we're nothing but trash."

"She didn't do nothing of the kind," Leah snapped. "Don't mind him, baby. He's had a bit to drink."

Hannah faced her father squarely but didn't say the obvious. He had consumed far more than a "bit" and that wasn't unusual. "I have to finish getting ready."

She went back to her bedroom and heard the argument start again. Nothing changed. Who had said you couldn't go home again? It was as if she had never left. For a moment she considered not going to the dance and heading back to Austin that very night. But she knew she couldn't miss the chance of seeing Trey again. Of dancing with him. Of being in his arms even if it was only on a dance floor. She put on her heels and picked up her purse.

She called out a good-bye to her mother but got no answer. The tempo of the argument had picked up considerably. Hannah went out and pulled the door shut behind her.

* * *

Across town Ruth McCullough was pacing in her sitting room. She wouldn't have called it pacing, but she was unable to sit still. She knew Trey was going to see the Branson girl.

Several times she had gone to the phone to call him and tell him not to believe a word that girl might say, but she had no reason to give as to why she thought it necessary to warn him. She had no choice but to remain quiet and worry that the girl might tell Trey the part his mother had played in her decision to leave town so suddenly and unexpectedly.

Ruth poured herself a brandy and tried to sit down and get interested in her needlepoint. She had thought everything would be all right when she had moved Hannah out of the picture at Trey's high-school graduation. Hannah had certainly been glad to take her up on her offer. Ruth had wished she could tell Trey just how eager Hannah had been to get out of Clearwater and consequently away from him. But that would have been impossible without admitting her offer.

Trey never had suspected his mother had had any part in Hannah's leaving. Ruth had to give the girl credit for that; she had lived up to her end of the bargain. She knew Hannah had been back to Clearwater at least a few times since, because she had seen her downtown shopping with her mother, but Hannah had never contacted Trey. Ruth didn't regret what she had done. After all, the girl had made something of herself, thanks to the

McCullough money. She was a doctor now and apparently well thought of in Austin. Ruth had friends there and had made discreet inquiries. After all, Hannah's career was an investment of sorts.

But now they would be together, and Ruth was deeply uneasy. The night couldn't have been more perfect for upsetting her plans. It was Valentine's weekend, for one thing, a day when most people thought, at least in passing, about romance. And they were going to a dance at the same location where they had attended their senior prom and countless other dances during their school years, and would probably be dancing to music that would trigger nostalgic memories. Ruth couldn't have been more distressed at their being together.

She still saw Amos Branson around town and occasionally Leah. Ruth had known them both all her life, though she never had passed more than a word or two with them in all that time. Branson was an even worse case than he had been fifteen years ago, though Ruth would have sworn at that time that it would have been impossible. Leah was decent enough, but she had stayed married to the town drunk, so Ruth had little respect for her. Ruth couldn't imagine how Leah had abided staying with a person like that. But then, Ruth had never been in Leah's place.

The chime of her grandfather clock told her it was getting late. Trey would be leaving soon. Was he going to pick Hannah up? Was it a genuine date? Ruth hadn't asked, and Trey hadn't volunteered any details. Ruth went to the phone and punched in Trey's number. She couldn't sit around and let all her plans be thrown away. If Hannah didn't turn Trey's head again, he might eventually acknowledge that his mother was right and remarry Eden Clark. Ruth had to do what she felt was in Trey's best interest. The phone rang again and again, but there was no answer. Ruth paced back to her chair and restlessly sat down. Trey was already gone. Gone to meet Hannah. She sipped her brandy and worried.

The evening was cooler than Hannah had expected, but rather than go back for her wrap, she continued across the porch and down the steps. She wanted to put as much distance between herself and her father as possible. It was visits like this that proved to her she had been right in accepting Ruth McCullough's offer. Time and distance sometimes dulled her memories of what it had been like to live here, but this weekend had brought it all into sharp focus.

She drove to the lake and parked in the lot beside the Pier House. When she opened her car door, she could hear strains of music drifting down from the ballroom on the top level of the building. It was as if she were hearing her prom music all over again. The tune was an old one that brought back waves of memories of Trey and her youth.

Trey was waiting for her on the veranda that wrapped around the building. "You're a little late. I was afraid you wouldn't come," he said when she drew near.

"I said I would be here."

"You look beautiful tonight. But then you always do."

Hannah smiled but had to remind her heart not to race at his compliments. "I might say the same about you. I thought maybe you'd be balding or developing a pot belly by now. Most of our classmates are."

"And that's only the women," he said with a laugh.

She smiled at his jest. "You haven't changed at all."

His smiled faded. "That's where you're wrong. I've changed a great deal. I know now that some things are worth whatever effort it takes to achieve them."

"Such as?"

"Such as us." He put his arm around her waist and drew her near. "When you called, it struck me how easily I might lose you again. All you had to do was to get into your car and drive away."

"You know I'm in Austin now. You even know I'm with St. Thomas Hospital. You could find me."

"But not if you didn't want to be found."

Hannah knew this was the time to tell him not to come in search of her, but she couldn't form the words.

Trey drew her closer. "Do you really want to go to the dance?"

She was about to shake her head when she heard Kit and Mike behind them.

"Hi," Kit said brightly. Then, "Are we interrupting something?"

"No. No, of course not," Hannah said quickly, backing away from Trey. "We were just going upstairs." Her eyes met Trey's and begged him to understand, but she couldn't tell if he did. She didn't trust herself to leave the dance and be with him, because she might never leave him at all.

They went upstairs, Trey and Mike talking about offshore fishing in Galveston and about how much Clearwater had changed through the years. Kit was telling her about her youngest son's latest escapade, but Hannah's mind was elsewhere. What would have happened if she had gone with Trey? She had broken his heart fifteen years ago. What could he feel for her now?

Like the brunch, Eden had been in charge of the dance arrangements and the ballroom reflected her touch. Hannah couldn't have said what the theme had been for her senior prom, but it all came back when she saw the room. "Do you suppose these are the same decorations?" she whispered to Trey. "It looks the same as it did for our prom!"

"Eden never quite grew up. She's still a cheer-leader at heart." Trey's voice held no animosity toward his ex-wife. He was only stating a fact.

The theme was "Over the Rainbow" and rainbows were everywhere. At eighteen Hannah had thought the room decorated this way had looked like a romantic fantasy; at thirty-three she would have preferred a more adult setting. The musicians, with the exception of one or two, were the same ones who had played at the senior prom. Now their hair was thinning and a few were graying but their music was still as good. "It's even the same band!"

"It's the only stage band in Clearwater. They played at all the school dances. All but two of the original musicians still live here and they hire out for most of the reunions." He led her to the dance floor.

Hannah felt her heart quicken as she stepped into his arms. This was dangerous territory for her. He felt far too good.

As a teenager, Trey had been an excellent danc-er, and it was clear that he hadn't lost his skill. They moved to the rhythm of the music as if they danced together every night. Hannah felt the beat move her, and she felt as if she were floating. There was a touch of fantasy about being here, dancing with Trey, beneath a mirrored ball that cast reflections of light around the room.

He was handsomer than ever. The years had taken away some of his certainty that he would always lead a charmed life and had left small lines that bracketed his mouth. His eyes now held a mysterious darkness as if he had known a deep hurt but had survived it and grown stronger because of it. She wondered if his divorce had put that look in his eyes. Had it been her leaving him? She ached to think she could have caused him even momentary pain.

"What are you thinking?" he asked.

"I was wondering about you. What you're like now, what your dreams are these days. I was wondering how much you've changed."

"We all change. I no longer dream of setting the world right. I'm doing all I can just to keep Clearwater on track." He grinned. "World conquering proved to be more of a challenge than I had thought it might be at eighteen."

She smiled up at him. "I know what you mean."

"I'd say my dreams are the same as most people's. I want to be happy and in love with a woman who loves me back. I'd like to have a family."

"And a house with a pool and two cars," she prompted. "You always used to say that."

"I already have that. What do you dream of achieving these days?"

"I want to be happy, too. And I'd like a family, but my biological clock is ticking, as they say. I've considered adoption."

"You have?"

"Single mothers adopt children these days. It's not all that unusual."

263

"Why haven't you?"

She looked away. "I'd like to have a complete family—father and all. And my schedule is hectic at times. I don't know if it would be unfair to a child."

"You're on call often? I don't know much about doctors' lives."

"Since I'm single, I take calls for some of the other doctors on weekends or holidays. I prefer to stay busy."

"It's harder to think that way."

"What do you mean by that?"

"I think you're still running from yourself."

Hannah stopped dancing and was nearly run over by another couple. "I'm not running from anything."

"No? I seem to have hit a nerve." Trey met her eyes squarely and his eyes seemed to read her thoughts.

Hannah went back into his arms. "That's ridiculous. I'm a good doctor."

"I'm sure you are. That's not what I meant and you know it."

"You're not in court. Stop cross-examining me." She moved with him to the music, wishing she could tell him the whole truth about her decision to leave Clearwater and him. "There were extenuating circumstances."

"Such as?"

"I already told you I'm not at liberty to discuss it."

"Hannah, that was fifteen years ago. What could you possibly not tell me at this date?"

She didn't answer. She couldn't tell him his mother was at the base of it all.

When the music ended, they walked off the dance floor. As the next song started, Trey seemed about to speak, but Eden came up and touched his elbow.

"Could I have this dance?" she said as if she were still a child in dancing class.

Trey looked as if he wanted to refuse, but Hannah sat down at the nearest table and waved at him in dismissal. She needed time to put everything in perspective. Dancing with Trey had left her more ambivalant than ever about her feelings for him.

Trey drew Eden into the dance steps. She looked up at him with a pout he had thought was cute at eighteen, but now it seemed silly.

"I think you're ignoring me," she said in her little-girl voice. "You walked right past me at the door and didn't even speak."

"I didn't see you." It was true. He had seen no one but Hannah. It had been that way all weekend.

"I can't tell you how proud I am that everything has worked out with the reunion. I've worked and worked for months!" She made it sound as if she had hung every rainbow and planned every moment singlehandedly.

"It's been successful," he said. "A lot of our classmates showed up."

"Of course they did. We had a very special class. None of the classes we knew were as closely knit. I still keep in touch with all the cheerleaders, naturally." She whispered, "Can you believe how much weight Sally Jean has put on? You'd think she would have gone on a diet since she knew we would all be seeing her."

"Maybe she has more important things to think about."

"Go ahead, cut me down. You always think you know more than anyone else." Eden pouted, but when Trey made no response, she changed her tactics. "I almost didn't recognize Hannah Branson."

"No?" Trey knew he would have recognized her anywhere, at any time.

"I've heard she's a nurse now."

"She's a doctor."

Eden frowned across the floor in Hannah's direction. "So she says. I never thought she would come this weekend."

"Why not?"

"Well, you know what her father is like! You can see him drunk every night of the week. He doesn't even pretend to hold down a job! I'd be too ashamed to show my face back here."

"Hannah isn't her father. You can't judge her by his actions."

"They say an apple doesn't fall far from the tree. Look, she's ordering a drink!"

"Eden, most of the people here are having a

drink." He wondered if the song would last for-ever. He wanted to go back to Hannah.

"Mark my words, she has something to hide."

He looked down at her. "Why do you say that?"

"Why, look at how she left all those years ago! You were as thick as thieves and all at once she was gone. She didn't give anyone an explanation or so much as a good-bye, from all I've heard. She just up and left town."

"She probably was eager to get away from all the gossips," he said pointedly.

"I don't doubt it," Eden said, not getting his point. "Everyone said she would never amount to anything. I'll bet she's not a doctor at all."

The music faded to a close and Trey was glad to lead Eden off the floor. He left her with a group at the edge of the dance floor and went to where Hannah was sitting.

"You two dance well together," she observed. "She's still beautiful."

"I don't want to talk about Eden."

"No?"

"I'd rather talk about you."

"There's nothing else to say about me."

"I feel as if there is. I have all these things I want to know and to tell you, and I can't seem to find a way to do it."

"Trey, we only have tonight. That's all we can ever have. Tomorrow I'm going back to Austin and my life there and you're staying here. We have other commitments and other people who depend on us and other plans for our futures."

"If we have only one night, I'm damned if I'm going to spend it dancing under crepe paper rainbows. Let's go for a walk."

Hannah knew she shouldn't, but she nodded.

They left the crowded room and went out onto the pier. Moonlight made a silvery path on the lake's gently undulating surface. Hannah smiled. "When I was a girl, I thought fairies could walk on moonbeam paths."

"They can't?" he said as if surprised.

She laughed. "It's been a strange weekend, hasn't it? Seeing all these people and recognizing them, but seeing how much we've all changed. It's sad and nice, all at the same time."

"All your improvements have been for the better. I do miss the freckles on your nose, however."

"They still make an appearance if I'm in the sun too much."

Trey took her hand and leaned back against the wooden rail. "I don't want you to go."

"You know I have to."

"I know, but I don't like it." He studied her hand and ran his thumb over it as if he were deep in thought.

Hannah felt the sting of tears and blinked to keep them from gathering. "I guess that's the problem with reunions. It's like traveling in a time machine. We forget we can't go back."

"I don't want to go back. Not if it means losing you all over again."

"It's not as if you've pined ever since. You've been married and built a successful career."

"I'm not the sort to pine away. That doesn't mean I wouldn't want it to be different if I could manage to change it."

"I had to leave, Trey. Seeing my father this weekend reminded me of how much I had to get away. You don't know what it was like. You couldn't possibly know."

"I can understand your wanting to leave your father's house. I can't understand why you also wanted to leave me."

She drew in a deep breath. He deserved some explanation. "Papa is drunk all the time. That's why I didn't want you to pick me up at the house. He and Mama were fighting, and I didn't want you to walk into it. Trey, if you could see what it's like, you wouldn't wonder at my having to leave town."

"You could have married me." He said the words simply, and she could hear the old hurt in his voice.

She was silent for a time. "I couldn't do that to you. I knew you planned to become a lawyer, and I thought I would be a hinderance to you."

"No, you wouldn't have been."

"Trey, be reasonable. You know how people in Clearwater see my father. I've lived under the shame of being Amos Branson's daughter all my life. I know it's not my imagination."

"We could have gone to live somewhere else. You could have still gone to medical school, but we would have been together."

"I guess I was too proud." She pulled her hand free and put it on the rail as she looked out over the water. "I was afraid I would be a liability to you, that I would hold you back. Your father was determined to have you in his law firm. He would never have forgiven me if you had moved away permanently because of me. And you might not have been able to become a lawyer, if we were married, or me a doctor. Babies have a way of coming along, and we might not have been able to have careers and a family as well. Not when we were both trying to get started."

"My career isn't the most important part of my life. Or at least I wish it weren't. I would have chosen you over it."

"I know. That's one reason I had to go."

"What's another?"

"Trey, it's so long ago. Why are we even discussing it?"

"Because I still love you."

She felt as if her breath were caught in her throat. She couldn't speak. She wanted to say she had never stopped loving him, but her promise to Trey's mother kept her silent.

"No comment? I'd have thought that would have elicited at least an 'oh?'"

"You caught me off balance. I never expected

you to say that." She gripped the rail as if she were afraid of spinning off into space. Trey still loved her!

He put his hands on her shoulders and gently turned her to face him. "Hannah, I know I'm taking a big chance by telling you how I feel. I'm afraid you'll dissolve like mist and be gone, but I have to say it. I've never stopped loving you, and I never will."

"You can't know that."

"Yes, I can. Are you saying you don't feel anything for me at all?"

Hannah could never tell a lie of that magnitude. The words would have choked her.

"Answer me. What do you feel for me?"

Her eyes met his, and she felt herself becoming lost in their depths. "I'll always love you, Trey. I could stop breathing before I could stop loving you." Her voice broke, and she could feel the tears well and spill over onto her cheeks.

Trey let out his breath as if he had been holding it in fear of what she might say. Silently, he drew her to him. For a long while, they held each other, feeling the heaven of their embrace and being fearful of losing it again.

"Will you marry me?" he asked, his lips against her hair.

Hannah felt her heart break as she shook her head. "I can't marry you."

Trey sighed as if he had expected her to say that. "Why?"

"So much has happened. We don't even know each other anymore."

"You know that's not true. It's as if we've never been apart."

"I have a life in Austin. Yours is here."

"People move all the time."

She lifted her face and tried to smile up at him. It was impossible. "I wouldn't be good for business. Our family gatherings would be nightmares."

"Then we won't gather with them. I love you, Hannah. I can't bear to lose you again."

"We may not have a choice," she whispered softly.

"You have to explain that. Hannah, don't turn away. I'm asking you to marry me. You can't just not answer."

Her tears flowed faster, and she wiped at them with her palm. "Trey, it's never been as simple as you think. We can't love each other. We certainly can't marry. We aren't just individuals. We have our families to think about."

"I can handle that. You aren't as tainted around here as you seem to think. At one time that might have been true, but Clearwater isn't as close-minded as it used to be."

"Your mother would never welcome me into your family."

"Mother? What does she have to do with this?"

Hannah pulled back from him. "I love you, Trey. If I could have, I'd never have left you in the first place. Don't ask me any more questions."

She saw him step forward and his mouth opened to speak. Tears blinded her, and she turned and ran. She couldn't see where she was going, but miraculously she didn't stumble and he didn't run after her. She fumbled her way into her car and drove until she was out of sight of the Pier House, then she stopped by the side of the road and cried until she felt drained and empty.

Chapter Five

Sunday

"Just go on back to Austin and don't bother to come back!" Amos shouted at his daughter. "We don't need you here and never have!"

"Amos, don't say stuff like that!" Leah protested. "Don't you pay him no mind, Hannah. He goes on like that sometimes."

"I'm leaving early," Hannah said. She couldn't feel anything today. Her father had been railing at her and her mother ever since she woke up, and she had found herself growing numb just as she had when she was a child to protect herself from the emotional pain. She didn't dare acknowledge that the night before was probably the last time she would ever see Trey.

"Good. And take your mama with you," Amos said as he noisily sipped his coffee laced with whiskey. "I don't need her here." His voice dropped to a grumble. "Always hanging around, telling me what to do. I don't need her!"

Hannah glanced at Leah. Her mother was sitting across from her, her face a careful mask. "Mama? Will you come back with me?"

"Can't." Leah bit a corner off her toast, keeping her eyes on her plate. "You know I have to work."

It was on the tip of Hannah's tongue to tell her father that if Leah hadn't been such a good provider, he wouldn't have had the luxury of lying around and drinking all the time, but she stopped herself. There was no point in making matters more stressful for her mother. She pushed her plate away. "I'm not hungry."

"Are you already packed?" Leah asked as Amos helped himself to more coffee and sloshed a generous amount on the counter top, without a thought of cleaning up after himself.

Hannah nodded. "I couldn't sleep. I've been up for a long time." How could she sleep knowing she would never see Trey again? He loved her. How much did she owe to a promise she had made as a desperate teenager?

The phone rang and her mother answered it. "It's for you, Hannah."

For a minute Hannah thought it must be Trey, then hoped it wasn't. Tentatively, she answered, surprised to find Ruth McCullough on the line. "Mrs. McCullough?"

"I'd like for you to come by here before you leave town."

Hannah paused. "All right." She couldn't imagine what Ruth could possibly want to talk to her about that couldn't be said over the phone. Against all reason, she felt hope rising. Was Ruth about to capitulate on her insistence that Hannah stay away from Trey?

When Hannah hung up, Leah was watching her expectantly. "That was Mrs. McCullough?"

Hannah nodded. "She wants me to come by there."

"Maybe she's gonna offer you a job scrubbing her baseboards," Amos said with a mean chuckle.

"I hardly think so." Hannah fixed him with a cool gaze. She knew about enabling and co-dependency, but she still couldn't reconcile her mother's willingness to stay married to a man as slovenly and abusive as her father.

Leah started carrying plates to the sink. "Today is Sunday. My day off. I wish you could stay a bit longer and visit a while. Seems like we haven't had a chance to really talk."

"I'd like to Mama," Hannah said with what was only half a lie. "I miss you."

Leah smiled and for a moment looked almost young and pretty. "I miss you, too, baby."

Hannah went to her bedroom, and as she picked up her suitcase, she noticed how incongruous the expensive piece of luggage looked in the threadbare room. She had already made up the bed and straightened the room from her visit. There was no reason to put off going back to Austin. Leaving her mother would be no less difficult for having put off the inevitable, and if she lingered, she was certain to have words with her father. She turned and walked into the living room. "I'm going, Mama."

Leah came in, drying her hands on the dish towel she was using as an apron. She hugged Hannah and kissed her cheek. "You drive careful now. You hear?"

"I always do." She hugged her mother. "If you get a chance to get away, call me and I'll send you money for a plane ticket."

"All right." They both knew that was a call Leah would never make.

Hannah called out, "'Bye, Papa." There was no reply.

"He probably didn't hear you," Leah said unconvincingly.

"Good-bye, Mama."

Hannah went out to the car and put her suitcase in the trunk. She always found it hard to leave. Not that the house or her father held any strings on her, but she worried so about her mother. Again she considered moving back to Clearwater. She would be near enough to check on her mother as often as she felt necessary and to see that she never wanted for anything.

With a sigh, Hannah started the car and waited

for some children playing in the street at the end of the driveway to move back into their yards before she backed out. The children were dirtier than any child could possibly have gotten so early in the morning, and even though the day was uncomfortably cool, they were all barefooted. There was a lot she might be able to do for the poor in Clearwater. As far as she knew, there was no free clinic here. The ones eligible for Medicaid had to go to the next town to get injections and check-ups for their children and not all of them had cars reliable enough to get them there.

Putting all that aside, she drove across town to the house where Trey had lived as a boy. She had never asked him where his house was now, and she wasn't sure she wasn't driving past it without even realizing it. No, she thought, she would somehow know if Trey was within a hundred yards of her. They had always had that curious chemistry between them.

Ruth McCullough's house was every bit as grand as were her neighbors' houses. There was money in Clearwater, due to the fact that it was so near the Kilgore oil field. The men who made their fortunes in oil, like the first Andrew McCullough, had preferred to live in the cleaner towns beyond the field, and thus, Clearwater had become home for a number of millionaires despite its size.

Hannah parked and walked up the front walk.

She had only been to this house one other time. Memories of that unpleasant day welled inside and threatened to overwhelm her. She rang the bell and waited.

Ruth opened the door and stepped aside for Hannah to enter. She felt the older woman's perusal but ignored it. She was no longer a child subject to intimidation. Ruth finally said, "I didn't know if you'd come."

"I said I would. I always do what I say I'll do." She met the woman's eyes levelly.

"Come into the sitting room."

Hannah followed her through a stiffly formal living room, large enough in itself to have contained Hannah's parents' house, and into a smaller and cozier room that had been a later addition to the house. Ruth sat in a well-padded chair and indicated Hannah should sit in the other. Instead, Hannah sat on the couch. It was a small rebellion, but she felt she needed all the edge she could get. "Why did you want me to come?"

"I thought we should talk. I know you've been in Clearwater a few times during the past fifteen years."

"Of course. My parents live here. Not seeing them was never part of our bargain."

"Certainly not. I only meant that until this weekend you have kept our agreement to stay away from Trey."

"This was a different circumstance. I was

attending my class reunion. That he also chose to attend wasn't my fault."

"Yet you apparently didn't avoid him. I know you had a date last night."

"Mrs. McCullough, I've lived up to our agreement for fifteen years. Trey and I are thirty-three years old. I think it's ludicrous for me to continue avoiding him. I've never stopped loving him, and I have reason to believe he loves me, too."

"You're wrong. I know my son as well as I know myself. He couldn't love you."

"No? He thinks he does."

Ruth let out an exasperated sigh. "Men will say anything. No, Trey and Eden are going to patch up their differences and remarry."

"Oh? That's news to Trey. He hardly spoke to her all weekend."

Ruth looked displeased. "That's because you were there. I want your promise to leave and not to try to see or speak to him again."

"I've done all you asked. I've tried to forget him. He has been married and divorced since I left Clearwater. Surely we've been through enough by now to do as we please." Hannah spread her hands. "Look at me. I've changed from the girl I was when I made that agreement with you."

"Thanks to me. Don't forget that."

"Thanks to you in part. I needed to get out of Clearwater and you gave me that chance. Without your financial support I might not have been able to break away. But then again, I might have. I never wanted to stay here. I wanted more for myself than my parents have. I might have been able to work my way through college and medical school. I'm grateful to you, but I'm not convinced that you were my only hope."

"That's all the gratitude I get?" Ruth was growing angrier and finding it hard to remain seated. "I put you through college, and you aren't even grateful?"

"I've said I'm grateful. But a promise such as you demanded was too high a price to pay in return. When I was eighteen, I thought my feelings for Trey would diminish over the years." She laughed mirthlessly. "I thought I would somehow not feel much of anything for him once I reached the great old age of thirty. Teenagers don't usually have much foresight. To promise not to see Trey forever was foolish of me."

"You promised! You said not ten minutes ago that you always keep your word."

"And I'm trying to do that. But Trey and I still love each other. I know you don't care about me, but don't you want to see your son happy?"

"My son is quite happy! Or at least he was before you came back!" Ruth shoved herself to her feet. "I should have known not to trust you! Andrew said you weren't to be trusted!"

"Neither of you knew me or what I was like. Your judgment of me was based on your prejudice against my father, and I resent that." Hannah remained seated but watched Ruth closely. Ruth was becoming extremely agitated.

Hannah heard a door closing somewhere in the back of the house and snapped her head around at the sound of Trey's voice. "Mother? Are you home?"

"It's my son!" Ruth glared at Hannah as if she felt Hannah was responsible for Trey's untimely arrival. "Does he know you're here?"

"Not yet."

Trey came into the room, and when he saw Hannah, he stopped in his tracks. "Hannah? What are you doing here?"

"She just dropped by," Ruth said unreasonably.

"I didn't know you two knew each other." Trey was looking from one to the other as if he were starting to put the clues together.

"We don't," Hannah said. "I was just telling her that." Hannah stood to leave. She didn't want to cause more trouble.

"Wait. Don't go. I was going to come to your house when I left here."

"I'm on my way out of town."

"Without saying good-bye?" he asked. "You'd leave without telling me you're going?"

"Let her go, son," Ruth advised. She stepped nearer and put her hand protectively on his arm. "Let her be on her way."

Trey moved away from his mother. "I think I need to know exactly why she's here. Mother?"

Ruth frowned, and her skin took on a grayish pallor. "It doesn't concern you. Hannah came by to pick up a bundle of used clothing I'm sending to her mother. That's all."

This was more than Hannah's pride could take. "That's not true."

"Then why are you here?" Trey's eyes commanded her to be honest with him."

"I'm here because your mother called and asked me to come over."

Ruth shook her head. "It's those old clothes," she protested. "I . . . I had to give them to someone, and I thought . . ."

"Mother, you don't have any reason to send old clothes or anything else to Leah Branson."

Ruth started wringing her hands and pacing from the door to the window and back again. "It's all her fault. She's trying to start trouble. I had hoped to spare you this, Trey. I'm only doing what is best for you."

"I think you'd better tell me the whole story." He looked at Hannah, but she shook her head.

"It has to come from your mother or it won't be said. I gave my word."

"I'm not leaving until I know what the hell is going on." He scowled at his mother. "Stop pacing and start talking."

"I tried to be her benefactor! Your father and I knew she would never amount to anything if she stayed here in Clearwater, so we arranged to send her away to college."

Trey stared at her, his face a mask of disbelief. "You and Father sent Hannah to college?"

"I put myself through medical school," Hannah put in quickly. "They paid for my bachelor degree."

"You never told me that." Trey wheeled on his mother. "Neither of you ever said a word about it to me."

"We didn't want you to know. It didn't concern you."

"Yes, it did," Hannah said. "This has gone on too long. If you don't tell him, I will."

"You keep quiet!" Ruth demanded. "Don't say another word!"

Trey's voice turned cold and brittle as he demanded, "Then you tell me. I'm waiting."

"We knew she was all wrong for you," Ruth said, her fingers wringing and plaiting together. "We knew you deserved better."

Hannah lifted her head as the barb struck home, but she said nothing.

"It was your father's idea originally. He mentioned that Hannah might leave you alone, if she were to go away to college—not to the University of Texas where you were going, but to some other one. I suggested we could pay for it as a condition of her not seeing you again. He thought that was a great idea."

"You paid Hannah to leave town and break up with me?" He looked at Hannah. "You agreed to that?"

"I thought I had no other choice," Hannah said in her own defense. "You were planning on leaving for four years of college, then law school. I couldn't stay here and wait. You know what Papa is like. I took the opportunity to leave, too. Besides, I also mistakenly believed her when she told me you wouldn't have anything else to do with me, even if I refused her offer and stayed. I know now I was wrong, but at the time I thought it was my only chance."

Trey glared at his mother. "You did this to us?"

"I did it for your own good!" Ruth stopped wringing her hands and began rubbing her upper chest and left shoulder, and she winced as if she was in pain. "I only did it because I love you. You're my only son!"

"Hannah, why didn't you tell me this?"

"I promised her I wouldn't," she said simply. "I gave my word."

Ruth's skin was growing grayer by the second. Grabbing her chest with both hands, she slumped to the floor. Hannah was at the woman's side at once. "Mrs. McCullough, speak to me. Where are you hurting?"

Ruth mumbled something unintelligible. Hannah helped her into the chair. "Trey! Call an ambulance! Hurry!" She started loosening Ruth's collar and belt. "Mrs. McCullough, talk to me. Tell me what's happening," Hannah said as she started taking Ruth's vital signs. She had the classic symptoms of a heart attack. "Talk to me! Don't you fade on me!"

Behind her, she could hear Trey punching in 911 and giving terse answers to the emergency operator. Hannah kept her fingers on Ruth's reedy pulse. "Trey, my car keys are in my purse. In the trunk beside my suitcase is a small black bag. I need it quickly." She had never lost the habit of carrying the bag with her to Clearwater even when she had no reason to believe she might need it. Her mother never saw a doctor, if she could help it, and Hannah wanted to be ready for any emergency.

Ruth's pulse skipped, and for a moment Hannah thought she might have lost her. She talked louder, not allowing Ruth to slip into unconsciousness. "Fight back, damn it! You're not going to leave us now!"

Trey came racing through the house, the black bag in his hand. Hannah grabbed it and yanked it open. She put on her stethoscope and listened to Ruth's heartbeat. She didn't like what she heard.

"How is she?" Trey asked. "What can I do?"

"Step out onto the porch and wave to the ambulance to help them be sure they have the right address." Hannah knew family members were of no help at a time like this.

Suddenly, Ruth flinched and her eyes opened wide. She lurched forward and her pulse and breathing stopped.

Hannah lost no time. She pulled Ruth down

onto the floor and began CPR. Where was the ambulance?

After what seemed to be an eternity, Hannah heard the faint sound of a siren. She continued to breathe for Ruth and pump blood through the woman's heart with rhythmic pressure on her chest between breaths. Hannah had seldom lost a patient, and she had no intention of losing this one—not even if the woman had stood between her and her happiness for nearly half her life. When she saw the EMTs, she said, "I'm a doctor. The patient is suffering a massive coronary!"

As the EMTs took over the CPR with an Ambu bag and oxygen, Hannah stood and drew a deep breath, flexing her aching arms and shoulders. Trey looked at her for instructions. "I'll ride in the ambulance with your mother," she said to him. "Are you all right to drive?"

"I have a pulse!" one of the EMTs said. "She's back."

Trey nodded to Hannah as they put his mother on a stretcher. "I'm okay."

Hannah hurried after the EMTs and Ruth. There was no time to think about herself or Trey. All her attention was focused on her patient.

The ride to the hospital was short, but it seemed to take forever. At one point, Ruth's pulse faded again and she stopped breathing, but Hannah and the EMT quickly resumed CPR, and before they got to the hospital, Ruth was again breathing on her own.

The McCulloughs' family doctor, Louis Farring, was waiting for them at the hospital's emergency-room entrance. "Doctor Branson," he said to Hannah by way of greeting as he nodded and took charge of his patient.

Hannah was surprised that Farring knew she was a doctor. She nodded back. "She's hanging in there."

At Dr. Farring's invitation, Hannah joined him in the emergency room to attend to Ruth, and she stayed with Ruth until she was on a heart monitor and her condition had stabilized.

Once Farring was satisfied the crisis had passed, he removed his stethoscope and said to Hannah in a low voice, "She's tough."

"You're telling me."

"It's a good thing you happened to be there. I hear you were giving CPR when the EMTs arrived. She would have died without your quick action," he said as he walked out with her into the hall.

Now that the emergency was over, Hannah had to have her curiosity satisfied. "Dr. Farring, how did you know I was a doctor? I'm sure we've never met."

"Trey mentioned that a doctor was with his mother when he called in that she'd had a heart attack. Of course, I didn't know it was you until I saw you getting out of the ambulance. But I already knew you'd become a doctor. Congratulations."

Hannah couldn't keep the surprise from her

face. She had no idea that Clearwater's most respected doctor had been keeping up with her. "Yes. I'm practicing in Austin."

"You wouldn't consider moving back here, would you? I know Clearwater can't offer the night life Austin has, but we sure need another doctor or two."

"That's what I hear." She looked down the hall to where Trey was waiting impatiently. "I'm giving it some thought."

"Clearwater needs some new blood. My partner will be retiring in a month or so, and there would be an opening in my office. I'd love to have you join me. Give it serious thought. Okay?"

She nodded, and after excusing herself, she headed down the hall toward Trey. He met her halfway. "Well?" he said.

"She's stabilized. All the indications are that she's going to make it."

Trey sighed with relief. "I thought she might not. We nearly lost her."

"She's a fighter. That's probably what saved her."

"That and the fact that you were there. I know she stopped breathing, Hannah. I'm not a fool. You saved her life."

"That's my job," she said as lightly as she could. "That's what doctors do."

"Why didn't you ever tell me she and Father were the reason you left me?"

"She made it a part of the agreement that you

were never to know anything about it. Don't blame her. She really thought she was saving you from a fate worse than death."

"How can you be so calm about it?"

"Because I've known about it for fifteen years, and I've had time to get used to the idea. You've only known a few minutes. And, besides, I've decided not to let that agreement ruin the rest of my life."

Trey studied her. "You must hate her for all she's done."

Hannah shook her head. "I don't hate her. She gave me a start in life, and she did it for you, as misguided as it might have been."

"So what happens now? Are you going to go back to Austin never to see me again?"

"You're not listening. I said I'm not going to abide by the agreement any longer. I owe her a great deal, but I just paid it back. She gave me a life and I gave her one. We're even."

Trey put his arms on her shoulders. "What are you saying?"

"Dr. Farring just offered me a position in his office. I told him I'd think it over."

"You're coming back to Clearwater?"

"It all depends on you. Do you still want to marry me, now that you know how your mother feels about me?"

For a minute Trey only looked at her, his face filled with wonder. Then his lips curved up in a smile, and he pulled her into his embrace. "I love

291

you, Hannah. Of course I still want to marry you. How can you even ask such a thing?"

She blinked to keep her tears from spilling over. "I want to marry you. I love you so much I ache for wanting to see you and to touch you."

He drew back and gazed into her eyes. "We've wasted too much time. You don't want a long engagement, do you?"

She shook her head, tears sparkling in her eyes. "I only need enough time to get out of the commitments I have in Austin. Then I'll be back."

He lowered his head and kissed her. His lips were warm and hungry on hers, and she responded with a passion that threatened to overwhelm her. She pulled back and glanced about to see if any of the hospital's staff was watching. Fortunately, the hall was still empty.

"Don't take too long in Austin," he said.

"I won't. And after this, I'll never leave you again."

Hand in hand they walked down the corridor so Trey could see for himself that his mother was out of danger. Hannah felt as if a tremendous burden had been lifted from her shoulders. As she watched Trey go to his mother's side and bend close to give her reassurance, she wondered what Ruth would have to say about her life being saved by Hannah Branson.

Ruth pulled Trey closer. Her lips moved before she could get the words out. "I was wrong," she whispered. "About Hannah."

Trey grinned and patted her hand. "I know. It's going to be okay now." Ruth closed her eyes, and he looked back at Hannah and winked. She returned the wink and smiled.

Chapter One

Linda Hepler was crying. This would have out-
raged anyone who knew her or knew about her
because she had no reason, no reason at all to cry.
It was true Linda was an orphan, but a most loving
aunt and uncle had substituted for her parents.
And the death of her parents before she knew or
could miss them had made her the mistress of a
most satisfactory fortune. In fact, Linda was both
beloved and rich.

Nor did she have the excuse for crying that she
was beloved because she was rich. Her aunt and
uncle were a great deal richer than she. What
was more, they had no children and Linda was
their heir.

Linda could not even call herself an ugly duck-
ling. Just now, with her nose and eyes red and

her soft brown hair mussed, she looked like a disheveled mouse. Under more normal conditions the sparkle of her big brown eyes and the upward curve of her pretty mouth made her piquantly attractive.

In fact, Linda was crying because she was young. She was crying because she had nothing to cry about. At the moment, she was bored to death. Life stretched ahead of her as a dull gray blank. The money and the love only wrapped her in a big, soft insulating cocoon that nothing could pierce. Even her wealthy and beloved friends had unhappy love affairs or troubles at home. She had not even pain or discomfort to interest her.

Auntie Evelyn and Uncle Abe were too perfect, she thought, sobbing harder. They adored her; they were warm and interested, but they did not smother her. They let her go when she wanted freedom and received her back with delight and affection when she was ready. "They even trust me," she moaned pitifully to herself—knowing that trust had held her back from the drugs and drink that were anodyne to the rich and the bored.

At last the utter ridiculousness of self-pity for such a reason checked the tears. With a little shuddering gasp, Linda lifted her face from the dampened pillows of the elegant sofa and sat upright. Her face was so flushed that she almost looked as if the rose damask of the sofa had bled into her cheeks.

"What I need," Linda muttered, "is a good kick in the behind and a face full of mud. . . ." The mutter trailed off as the word brought a remark of Aunt Evelyn's to mind.

"We never get bored," her aunt had said, laughing. "Abe and I, like your dad, started out in the dirt, a couple of worms, squirming away from the big guys' feet."

"What I need"—Linda never minded talking to herself—"is a worm's eye view of life."

I'll fly home and get a job, she thought, still sniffing but already happier. Then her brightening eyes dulled again. That wouldn't really help. She'd still be wrapped in the cocoon. Even if she could bring Aunt Evelyn and Uncle Abe to understand that she wanted to find her own position, just as if she had no connections, and live on the salary she made, Arthur Gelhorn would find her.

That was a sobering thought. Arthur was easy to resist now because she simply wasn't interested. If she accomplished her purpose and got a good mouthful of mud, Arthur might look desirable by comparison. Aside from that, if her uncle and aunt were too close by, it would be too easy to give up as soon as life got a bit unpleasant. Of course, London was no more than a phone call or a plane ride from New York, but psychologically there was a greater separation. Here in London, Linda thought, her eyes getting brighter and brighter, I wouldn't have to explain anything to anyone. All

Roberta Gellis

I'd have to do, is write home, say I felt bored and decided to take a job.

No one would have to know anything—that she was taking pay instead of being an unpaid volunteer, as usual; that she was living on the pay. Linda's lips curved into a mischevious smile and the pink faded from her pert nose, restoring her charm. She moved to the graceful Chippendale writing desk, drew a sheet of hotel stationery from it, and began to write swiftly. Her letter was quickly finished, and she picked up the phone and asked for a porter to mail it and bring her a newspaper. Lots of things had changed in London, but the service in Claridges had not. In ten minutes Linda was again curled up on the sofa, but this time she was bright and cheerful, perusing the want ads.

Soon a frown dimmed the bright expectancy of her expression. There were problems she had not considered. England had a surplus of employable people and Linda had a dearth of practical skills and experience. The latter would eliminate the possibility of getting work as a secretary or salesgirl—most of the ads—and the former would make the authorities reluctant to provide her with permission to work, particularly when her financial condition did not merit special exemption.

With dimming hope she scanned the wanted columns. Really there was nothing. Disappointed, she turned the page idly and there, at the bottom of the column devoted to Household Help was:

"Wanted—Companion. A young, healthy, well-educated woman desired as traveling companion for elderly lady. No nursing or other experience necessary."

Linda stared at the name and phone number. Certainly she met the requirements and very likely, since Mrs. Bates intended to travel, it would not matter that she did not have a working visa. Linda's even teeth caught her full lower lip and nibbled it gently. She had wanted a worm's eye view of life, but did she want to be as much of a worm as a paid companion was?

A momentary qualm of indecision dissolved into a delighted chuckle. In for a penny, in for a pound—picking and choosing would not be possible to someone who *needed* a job. If her choice was between companion and waitress, then companion she would be, and for long enough to appreciate from the heart what now induced tears of boredom in her.

Now there was a lot to do. Linda sprang up, threw on a coat, grabbed her purse, and danced with impatience while she waited for the elevator. On the sidewalk she paused as the commission-aire asked, "Cab, miss?"

"Yes," Linda replied, and then, "No, thank you. I think I'll walk."

Poor girls looking for work did not enjoy the luxury of cabs. As she set off down the street, Linda's eyes narrowed. If she had been a working girl and lost her job, how much would she have to live on? A few hundred pounds to a few thousand in the bank. Not a sum to be squandered on cabs. That habit had to be broken at once.

Her walk soon took her to Oxford Street. A middle-class emporium provided a wardrobe that would not betray her. Linda made a mental note that almost all the new things would have to be washed at least once right away because to have all new clothing would be suspicious. But I'll have time, she thought. I won't get this first job.

The next step was to find a room. One could not go job hunting and give one's address as Claridges. Linda didn't even know where to look, but common sense took her by the underground to Victoria Station, where Information directed her to a tourists' aid booth and a list of bed and breakfast places. She found a room in a small private hotel not far from Earl's Court. By then it was too late to make a call to Mrs. Bates, but Linda was not discouraged. Whether or not she got that job, everything she had done was necessary background. She had made an excellent start.

Leaving her purchases in the newly rented room, Linda prepared to close the door—at least temporarily—on her past life. The first bitter pill she had to swallow was repressing the temptation to take a cab back to Claridges because she was getting very tired. Second thoughts were beginning to gnaw at her, but she set her jaw and packed her clothing into her large cases, placing only her underthings in a used valise she had purchased in a second-hand store near Victoria Station. Then she paid her bill.

Linda started to slip the charge card into her purse as she walked toward the bell captain, then stared down at it. With a hollow, frightened feeling, she went to the writing room, wrapped the charge card in a sheet of paper, and sealed it in an envelope. After she had locked the envelope into one of her cases, she requested the bell captain to store her things and arrange to have her mail kept for her. This time, when she walked out with the worn valise in her hand, the commissionaire looked at her very peculiarly as she refused a cab. It was not his business to interfere with guests, however, and he merely watched as she walked slowly away.

The fun had gone out of the enterprise, but Linda went along grimly, switching her valise from hand to hand. Down the steps and onto the train. What a relief to sit down. Change trains. It seemed a mile along the platform, and the steps to the next line looked like Mount Everest. Ah, a blessed seat again. As she emerged into the chill dark, Linda's lips quivered. It was an awfully lonely feeling to be trudging along with her valise to a small, ugly room. She stopped for a moment to rest and looked around, her stomach tying itself into knots.

Then, if she had not been afraid that the passersby would think she was mad, Linda would have laughed aloud. Of course she felt terrible and her stomach was in knots. Here it was after eight o'clock and she hadn't had a thing to eat since nine in the morning. There was a restaurant half a street along. Linda peered into the window and giggled. Not cordon bleu, she guessed, but she could bet that her appetite would be better than for many more elegant meals she had eaten.

The next morning Linda was surprised at her feeling of anxiety when her coins went into the call box. Her heart beat faster and her voice was a little breathless as she identified herself and the reason for her call and asked to speak to Mrs. Bates. A thin, sweet voice replaced the maid's cockney.

"Yes, this is Mrs. Bates."

"My name is Linda Hepler, and I am calling in answer to your advertisement for a companion. Has the position been filled?"

"No, it has not. How old are you, Miss Hepler?"

"I am twenty-five, Mrs. Bates. I am in good health and I have a bachelor's degree in literature. I hope that I will be suitable for the position."

"You are not an Englishwoman, are you? Are you Canadian?"

For a moment, Linda thought of telling a fib. Then she realized it was impossible. She had to offer identification. "No," she said, "I am an American, but—"

"American? Why—"

The coin Linda had inserted fell, signaling that time had almost run out. Quick to seize opportunity, Linda said, "Oh, Mrs. Bates, I am so sorry. I don't have another coin. May I call you back in—"

"Never mind, Miss Hepler."

Linda's heart sank. She thought she had outfoxed herself, giving an impression of inefficiency by neglecting to provide herself with extra coins.

However, Mrs. Bates continued, "It would be better if you came round to see me. I am at Eleven Queen Street. Come at four. Goodbye."

It was amazing, Linda thought, as she replaced the phone, how a shoddy room, having to get up and come down for an ill-served and ill-cooked breakfast, and not being able to get room service or maid service to pamper every whim altered one's point of view. In spite of being intellectually aware of security, her emotional response was anxiety. She wanted that job almost as desperately as a girl without resources. Perhaps she wanted it even more desperately, Linda decided after mulling matters over, because she wasn't used to insecurity.

Returning to her room, Linda divided her time between looking at the "Companion Wanted" ads in the selection of newspapers she had purchased and washing her new clothes so they would not look too new. She marked a few other ads as possibilities, but did not phone. They were all companions to invalids, and Linda did not really want that kind of position. As she draped her wash-and-wear garments on strings tied here and there in her room, she found herself praying that she would suit Mrs. Bates.

Chapter Two

At precisely four o'clock, Linda was ushered into an apartment of delicate Edwardian elegance. There was nothing faded about it, however. It was apparent in the recently recovered seats of damask blue, the polished wood and sparkling glass that Mrs. Bates had money to spend and kept her pre-World War I furniture because she loved it.

"Miss Hepler, madam," the maid announced, and backed out, closing the door.

A small, slightly plump woman got spryly to her feet and came forward with a smile. "Good afternoon, Miss Hepler. Come and sit down. You are very prompt." The voice, high and almost too sweet, was unmistakable.

"Yes." Linda smiled, but she didn't fail to notice the old-fashioned lack of contractions in Mrs.

Roberta Gellis

Bates's speech. "To tell the truth, I have been waiting outside for over fifteen minutes. I was not quite sure how to get here and did not want to be late, so I was rather early."

Mrs. Bates laughed. "You should have come up at once. You must be chilled. Would you like some tea?"

Linda was pleasantly surprised. The saccharine quality of the voice had given her a qualm of uneasiness, but the offer and manner were truly kind. "Yes, indeed, I should like some very much. Thank you."

"Some Americans do not like tea," Mrs. Bates commented as she gestured Linda to a seat near a small table set with a variety of cakes and small sandwiches as well as cups and saucers and a china tea service of exquisite delicacy. "Will you pour, please."

"Certainly," Linda replied.

Mrs. Bates was apparently cleverer than she looked. Her round blue eyes under silky white hair drawn back into a graceful bun, which was obviously the work of a skillful hairdresser, gave her an appearance of innocence. Nevertheless the invitation to tea was a test as well as a kindness. Linda blessed the expensive finishing school she had attended before college, which still stressed such unfashionable arts as pouring tea and curtsying to royalty.

"Milk or lemon?" Linda inquired, with the teapot poised above a steadily held cup and saucer.

"Neither, thank you, but I like it very weak." A naughty smile made Mrs. Bates look like a kewpie doll. "I'm not supposed to have any, but I love it so."

Linda poured a small amount of tea concentrate into the cup; added hot water from the large pot. "I hope," she said, smiling ruefully, "that it will not be my responsibility to check your indulgence. I will admit right now that I should give in at once and be useless. Will you take sugar?"

"Saccharine, please—those little pills—two." Mrs. Bates watched Linda set the heavy hot water pot down gently, still holding the teacup, and pick out two saccharine tablets with the tiny tongs provided. She did not stir the tea, but placed a spoon in the saucer and handed the cup across. Mrs. Bates could not resist an approving nod, which gave away her thought that Linda was a well brought-up girl.

"No, you would not be expected to keep me in order. I am quite compos mentis. Your duties will be just what I said—to be a companion to me, help entertain my guests, make travel arrangements, write letters, and keep my social engagements straight—things like that."

"Well, I am sure I could do that efficiently, Mrs. Bates. I can type, although not really well enough to qualify me as a secretary or typist, and I am quite orderly. I like people, and I like to travel."

"That sounds very promising, Miss Hepler. Perhaps you would be willing to tell me something about yourself—about your experience and background."

Linda took a sip of the tea she had poured for herself as a delaying tactic. Up to this moment she had been speaking only the truth and she knew her manner was easy and natural. Now she had to begin on the tissue of half-truths and evasions she had worked out to support her tale of needing a job. Linda did not like to lie. She was afraid it would show in her face. She began with another completely truthful remark.

"I'm afraid I have no experience as a companion at all. Your advertisements said—"

"Yes, I remember. I said no experience was necessary. I didn't mean experience as a companion. You must have done some kind of work after your university graduation, however."

That was just what Linda had not done. Aside from charity work, she had simply lived on her very generous income, but she had known that this question would be asked and had planned an answer.

"Actually, I have done very little. I worked as a social secretary for a charitable organization—the March of Dimes—for a little while. But then an insurance policy left to me by my parents came due and I decided to spend a year or two seeing the world before I really settled down. Unfortunately—"

"Are you an orphan, my dear?"

"My parents died when I was very young. I do not even remember them."

"Poor child. But—"

The door sprang open, interrupting Mrs. Bates, to reveal a tall, gangling, extremely untidy young man. "Aunt Em," he said sharply, "I thought we had decided that I would find a companion for you."

Linda was startled, and when she looked at Mrs. Bates she was startled again because the old woman looked frightened. A moment later, however, it seemed she must have been mistaken because Mrs. Bates smiled.

"It's very good of you, dear, but when I thought it over, I decided I could suit myself best myself."

"But why, Aunt Em?" the young man asked in an exasperated tone, running a hand though his already untidy hair until it looked like a dust mop.

Linda lowered her eyes to her teacup. The question was ridiculous. Mrs. Bates had answered it before it was asked.

As if he had heard what his aunt said half a beat too late, the young man continued, "Why should you go through all the bother? You know you tire easily and all those phone calls and interviews— I'll bet you haven't had a moment's peace since that ad appeared."

"But it hasn't been a bother at all," Mrs. Bates said, smiling with determined sweetness. "I have quite enjoyed it. And after all, I'm sure it is all your fault."

"My fault?"

Mrs. Bates raised her brows. "If you did not tell Rose-Anne and Donald, I cannot imagine how they discovered I wanted a companion. They came up Wednesday and offered to find one for me."

An arrested expression froze the young man's mobile face. He shook his head. "You're a card, Aunt Em. There's no saying you aren't."

"After all," Mrs. Bates said cajolingly, "I could not show favoritism, could I? If I accepted someone you presented to me, Rose-Anne would be so hurt. And Donald would go about sneering more than ever."

"Okay. You did right. I've found just the right woman for you, too. All you have to do is say she answered your ad, and we won't have any trouble."

Linda, quietly sipping her tea, was furious. She could have wept with frustration, too. It seemed to her that she had been making headway. Mrs. Bates was just the type to be sorry for a poor orphan. And when she explained that she had stretched her insurance policy too far and was now nearly without funds—the reason she had decided on for seeking employment—she was sure Mrs. Bates would hire her without expecting references to be offered immediately. Now all her plans had been upset by this gangling, overbearing idiot.

"But I can't hire her," Mrs. Bates was saying, almost tearfully. "I have just engaged Miss Hepler."

Linda's eyes flew to Mrs. Bates, who had just turned away from her nephew, and met a decidedly pleading expression. Before she could speak, however, Mrs. Bates continued more firmly.

"I'm sorry, Peter. You will just have to explain that the position was already filled. I don't want a middle-aged woman with corns who has spent her life as a companion, who will sigh every time I want an errand run and who 'knows what is expected of her.' I want a young girl who is full of energy, who has a fresh mind and will enjoy going places and doing things and meeting people."

She put out a hand, and Linda put hers into it at once. "I like Linda, and I think she likes me."

"Indeed, I do, Mrs. Bates," Linda replied quietly, raising her eyes challengingly to the obnoxious Peter. . . .

WHILE THE FIRE RAGES
AMII LORIN

Winner Of Two *Romantic Times* Reviewers' Choice Awards!

An executive in charge of the multimillion-dollar Renninger hotel operation, Jo Lawrence is used to dealing with difficult people. But when her boss dies in a car accident, and his moody arrogant brother takes charge, her life turns upside down.

Charming and attentive one minute, angry and suspicious the next, Brett Renninger is impossible to work for—and even more impossible to resist. Despite the intoxicating madness Brett's passionate kisses rouse in her, Jo feels that he is holding something back from her. And when she decides to gamble her heart on the tender tyrant, she fears that Brett's secrets will destroy their chance at everlasting love.

_3369-0 $3.99 US/$4.99 CAN